A HEAVENLY CHRISTMAS

PATRICE WILTON

Published by Dreamscape Press

Copyright © 2015 Patrice Wilton
All rights reserved.
ISBN: 0-9912770-8-2
ISBN-13: 978-0-9912770-8-7

Other books by Patrice Wilton

REPLACING BARNIE
—book one in the Candy Bar series

WHERE WISHES COME TRUE
—book two in the Candy Bar series

NIGHT MUSIC
—book three in the Candy Bar series

REVENGE IS SWEET
—single title Women's Fiction

CHAMPAGNE FOR TWO
—single title Contemporary Romance

ALL OF ME
—single title Women's Fiction

A HERO LIES WITHIN
—Contemporary Romance

HANDLE WITH CARE
—Contemporary Romance

AT FIRST SIGHT
—Contemporary Romance

SERENDIPITY FALLS
—book one in the Serendipity Falls series

A COUGAR FOR KYLE
—book three in the Serendipity Falls series
—coming soon

DEDICATION

I would like to thank CommunityAuthors.com, and in particular my editor, Traci Hall for brainstorming with me and doing a wonderful editing job, and Christopher Hawke for his work creating my manuscript into print book format.

On a personal note, I'd also like to thank my partner, Ralph, for his patience when I'm working long hours each day and constantly obsessing over my book, and lastly, love to all my family, and hugs and kisses to my darling grandchildren.

CHAPTER ONE

Jennie Braxton opened her eyes slowly, but it was like fighting to swim upstream. She blinked, then blinked again. *Where am I?* The haze slid away and a face came into focus as it loomed in front of her. Deep brown eyes, a strong nose, and a cleft in his smooth chin. She didn't know him; she would have remembered someone as attractive as this.

"Ma'am?" He touched her shoulder. "Are you all right? Can you hear me?"

Her head hurt and she felt a little woozy. *What happened?* She nodded, but that caused a pain right between her eyes and she winced. "Yes." Jennie swallowed, her mouth dry. "Where am I?"

"You're in Heaven, ma'am." He smiled as if that was a good thing. "There was an accident."

"Heaven?" She tried to piece her memories together. An accident? *Am I dead?* "But my head hurts."

He nodded, his eyes warm with understanding. *So this is heaven.* Didn't seem too bad. This stranger made her feel safe, as if he saw everything clearly, like he knew things she had yet to learn.

Jennie nearly surrendered to the comfort offered in those beautiful brown eyes. Had she already passed the Pearly Gates? She didn't remember any bright light leading her heavenward. But she couldn't remember much at all.

He knelt so they were eye to eye. "You hit your head on the steering wheel. You ran into a tree."

Oh, God. Her stomach clenched as memories flashed through her mind—she was driving to her parents, the weather was bad. It had been snowing, the girls singing Christmas carols... The girls! "My children," she choked on the words and tried to move, but he kept his hand on her shoulder. "Are...are they here with me?" *No!* They were no more than babies. Only five and seven. It was too soon for them to see their daddy again. They deserved a life!

"Yes, but they're fine. Not a scratch." He smiled and glanced over his shoulder. She followed his gaze. Her children stood in the snow, looking like two little Elves dressed in their matching red and green striped leggings, their bright Christmas sweaters. A small Dalmatian pup was squirming in their hands, struggling to break free.

Relief rushed over her in a hot wave. Her daughters were alive. Jennie blinked away tears. Oh, thank the dear Lord! She whipped her head around—the movement causing her a sharp stab of pain. She was still in her car. It smelled like snow and pine trees and coffee. Earthly sights and smells. "I don't understand. How can this be heaven, if I'm in a car and they're not hurt?"

He laughed, his eyes crinkling at the corners, his full mouth resting in a smile. "You're in Heaven, Pennsylvania."

Jennie closed her eyes and took in the news. It was cold because he had the car door open. It smelled like coffee because she'd spilled her mug. "Oh. That *is* good." Her front window was cracked and the heavy pine scent came from the branch in her passenger side. "No wonder I hurt." She touched her forehead and felt something sticky.

"Katie? Brooke," she called to her children, needing to feel their warm, sweet bodies, to reassure herself that they were truly alive and well. The nice man leaned back as her daughters rushed forward. She'd lost enough in this past year, and if she'd lost them too. Well, it was unbearable. She couldn't, wouldn't, think about that.

"Mommy, are you okay?" Katie poked her head in and looked at her. Her daughter's eyes were a golden shade of brown, and right now they were wide with fear. "You scared us. You wouldn't wake up." She bit her lip, having learned too young about loss.

Jennie's head throbbed, but it was a minor problem compared to what could have been. "I'm fine, sweetheart."

"Good." Katie moved away from the door so Brooke could see into the car. Her five-year-old held the wriggling black and white dog and wore a big grin. "Look at the puppy. He's so cute." Brooke squealed as it tugged on her auburn braid like a chew toy.

The dog. More memories came back, like flashing headlights. Jennie had pulled off the highway, needing gas and a bathroom break. It was snowing, but not a heavy snow. Big, fluffy flakes. She had made the turn and was easing into the station when *that dog* ran in front of her car. She'd stomped on her brakes, swerved into a tree, and that's the last thing she remembered until she woke up with a stranger's face peering into hers.

"Help me out?" she asked him.

He rubbed the cleft in his smooth chin and shook his head. "The gas station owner called 911 and the ambulance is on the way. The police have been notified too."

She nodded. "Yes, but my children need me."

"You were knocked unconscious, ma'am, which means it's probably a concussion. The medics will want to check you out."

"I need to hold my kids." Jennie heard them playing with the puppy and knew they were fine, but she wanted them in her arms anyway. She undid her seatbelt, wondering why the airbags in her car hadn't deployed. Her stomach rolled at the smear of blood on the steering wheel. "Please?" She tried to push herself out of the seat, but the stranger's gentle grip was stronger than it seemed and kept her in place.

"I can't, ma'am. You wouldn't be here right now if I hadn't been chasing the puppy, trying to catch him so he wouldn't get hurt. I'm responsible for you."

She heard sirens and knew the ambulance was close. But before they came and whisked her away, she needed to feel her children safe in her arms. "Just one second with my girls."

He glanced at the kids and back at her. "Girls!" he called out. "Come give your mother a hug."

"I'm sorry," he said, "but what are your names?"

The girls dropped the dog as the ambulance pulled off the highway. They had been fine a minute ago but now they both burst into tears and squeezed between the door, the stranger and her lap. "This is Katie, and my youngest is Brooke. I'm Jennie."

"I'm Nick Ryan," he said, stepping away to give the girls more space.

She kissed their cheeks, and tasted their salty tears. "I love you both so much. If anything happened to you…" Jennie bit back a sob. She said a prayer of thanks and hugged them tight. Life was fleeting, fragile. Had Daniel been looking out for them tonight? A guardian angel?

Her husband had been a naval officer in Norfolk, Virginia on a training exercise when his helicopter went down. It was in January, almost a year ago.

"Don't cry, Mommy," Katie said, frowning at Jennie's forehead. "We'll take care of you."

She forced a smile and ignored the stabbing pain in her temple. "I know you will. You're the best girls in the world."

"Oh, oh." Brooke pushed out of her arms. "We forgot the dog. He's running away." Katie left her embrace too, in an eager attempt to catch the dog. The bad pup raced by the car, wagging his tail and running toward the gas pumps.

Nick leaned in, as if sensing how she must feel being deserted for an unknown pup. "You know kids," he said. "They can't sit still."

9

She swallowed a lump in her throat. "Yeah. I know. Hope you catch your dog." Jennie glanced at him, wondering why he hadn't had the pup on a leash. The accident could have been avoided.

"That's not *my* dog," he said with a shrug and a crooked grin. "I was on my way to work and saw him running down the road. I gave chase, trying to save him from getting run over, and darn near got you all killed instead." He glanced at her head injury and frowned. "I am so sorry, Jennie."

She sniffed. Whatever was he wearing? He smelled, well, heavenly. She turned her head and buried her nose in his collar, and sniffed again. His scent was a mixture of sweat and cologne. *Manly*. Why she could appreciate this now was beyond her. Could be the emotional state she was in after crashing into a tree, or the simple fact she hadn't been touched by a man in a year. She hadn't been aware that she'd missed it.

"And don't worry about the bills," the nice smelling man named Nick said. "I'll take care of everything."

"You don't need to do that," she answered. "I'm not destitute. Not yet, anyway. I have insurance, too." She gave a brief smile. "I don't want to go to the hospital. Would you do me a huge favor and tell the ambulance driver that I'm fine?"

"Nope. Listen, have them check you over and if the hospital releases you, call me and I'll drive you to the Inn. We only have one in town and they always have room. But I'm not going to let you sign off." He shifted so they were practically nose to nose and spoke quietly. "I'm not being obstinate, just practical. Years ago a buddy of mine had a sister, and she was skiing in Aspen during Spring break. She took a bad fall, and allowed the ski patrol to take her down the mountain, but then she refused treatment." His expression darkened. "She never made it through the night."

"That's a terrible story." She touched her throbbing head. "You win. I'll go. For everyone's peace of mind," she added, holding his gaze. He had a very caring face. Like Daniel's, she thought. A face that she had loved with everything in her heart.

"Thank you." He leaned back, giving her some room to breathe. "So where were you headed before I messed up your plans?"

"Philadelphia. To spend the holidays with my parents." She sighed. "We were almost there, but I was low on gas and the girls needed a bathroom."

He dug into the front pocket of his black winter coat and pulled out a phone. "Give me their number and I'll call them."

"That's kind of you, but if I could have my phone, I could do it." She glanced around. "I don't see it." Panic rose in her voice. Tears weren't far away.

Nick cleared his throat and she looked up into his warm brown eyes. "We'll find your phone later. Is there anyone else I should let know? A husband? The girls' father?"

"No." She took a calming breath, holding herself together. "Just my parents. John and Louise Howard."

Before she could say more, the ambulance arrived. Uniformed medics carried a stretcher toward her. She

11

wouldn't refuse treatment. She was a single parent now, and couldn't afford to take any chances.

Nick stepped away, allowing the two young men to take over. "I'll meet you at the hospital," he told her. "Don't worry. I'll call your parents and take care of the car. Everything will be fine."

"Thanks." She nodded and spoke to the medics. "The kids…Can they ride in the ambulance with me?"

"Yes, ma'am. They should be looked at too." Carefully, they lifted her onto the stretcher, asking her routine questions. Katie grabbed Jennie's purse from the car, brushing broken glass from the strap. Brooke carried her and Katie's backpacks. Jennie gave the medics the information they requested, and then she and the girls were lifted into the ambulance.

The last thing Jennie saw before they closed the ambulance door was Nick sneaking up behind the pup, grabbing hold of him tight, and then cradling him in his arms.

CHAPTER TWO

The ER wasn't busy when the ambulance arrived, and they were seen right away. Within an hour, Dr. Sue had pronounced the girls healthy, but told Jennie she wanted her overnight for observation. The three of them were in a brightly lit area, waiting for an available room. There was a small TV, a coffee station, a cold drink dispenser, and tables with magazines. It wasn't the Ritz but it was warm and reasonably comfortable.

A short time later, Nick entered. His black coat was undone, his cheeks flushed and raw from the cold. His dark hair was flecked with melting snow, but he wore a warm smile. "I called your parents. They are on their way. And the police arrived just after you were taken away so I let them know that I witnessed the whole thing. Gave them an accurate report of the accident, but you'll have to give them your insurance info when you get out of here." He ran a hand through his damp hair, shaking the snow off his shoulders. "Oh, and the garage towed your car to the body shop. I brought you your bag as well. It's still in my car. Figured you might need it."

"You did all that?" Tears welled and she sniffed them away. "How did you get their number?" she asked. "I never had time to give it to you."

"You said they lived in Philly, and you gave me both their names. Luckily they didn't have an unlisted number."

"Well, that was very kind of you." She gave him a weak smile. "I must have left my phone in the car. It was in the middle console."

"I found it." He pulled it from his jeans pocket and handed it to her. "Not sure if it's going to work. Looks a little banged up."

"Thank you," she said, looking at the smashed face. A phone could be replaced. A person—not so much. She turned it on and was pleased to see that it was still in working order.

"Nana and Papa are coming here?" Katie said, looking up from a book she'd taken out of her backpack. The girls were sharing a small bag of Cheetos Crunch and their fingers were a nice shade of orange. She brushed her hands on her corduroy skirt, and Jennie pretended not to see. "Can we all go home with them?" She asked with bright eyes and a happy smile.

"I wish we could, sweetheart." Jennie glanced from her daughters to Nick. "The doctor wants to keep me for tonight," she said, knowing she had to do whatever it took to be healthy and safe. Reaching for Brooke's hand, she wiped the fingers with a tissue from her bag, and added, "But you girls can go with them, and I'll join you tomorrow."

"Why can't you come too?" Brooke asked with a pout. "That's just mean."

"Not mean, honey. We're making sure that my head is all right." She touched the small bandage on her forehead, grateful it wasn't worse.

"Still think it's mean." Brooke rested her head on Jennie's lap. Poor sweetheart was tired after a long day and the trauma from the accident, she thought, tucking an auburn tendril behind her small ear.

Nick sat down in a chair, leaving space for her daughters. "Hey, I can drive you to Philly after you get out of here tomorrow," he said. "Your car won't be ready for several days. I mean, I'm no mechanic, but it's a mess."

"I'll rent something." She studied him, seeing his guilt and finding it unnecessary. "You don't need to hang around or pick me up. You've been kind enough," she said, wishing he'd go away so she and the girls could relax.

"I'll leave when your parents get here," he said, and took off his coat, sliding it onto a spare chair.

Jennie frowned. She hated the fact that she was forced to stay here a night, when all she wanted to do was get home with her parents and let her mother take care of her and the girls the way she loved to do. Every cell in her body ached. Her muscles were knotted and tight. Her head hurt. She wanted a good cry.

She knew that she must look hideous. Normally she considered herself reasonably attractive with her big green eyes, upturned nose, and shoulder length auburn hair. She was slim and athletic in build, five foot eight, and at thirty-one and a mother of two, she didn't look much different than when she was a flight attendant flying the friendly skies. Now? She felt nasty, wanting to brush her teeth and get the blood out of her hair.

Nick's blue sweater hugged his chest and he was wearing snug Levi's. His dark hair, worn on the longish side, waved around his ears, not like a barber shop cut, more like a salon. "Weren't you on your way to work?" She hoped he wasn't so busy feeling bad that he screwed up his job. "What do you do?"

He grinned and sat forward, his elbows on his knees. "I own a restaurant on Main Street. I'm a chef."

She checked out his hands and noted the long fingers with short nails. "Oh." Jennie was saved from clever conversation when she spotted her mom and dad coming down the corridor. He turned when he heard their voices and got up from his chair. She hadn't realized he was so tall before.

"Nana!" Katie set her book down next to Nick, and Brooke jumped off her chair beside Jennie. Both girls went barreling toward their grandmother. Dropping to her knees, the stylish sixty-year-old cuddled them close.

Jennie figured her mom would never really age. Louise Howard kept her hair a silvery blonde and stayed thin from the gym three times a week. Blinking away tears, Jennie noticed how frail and old her dad looked in comparison. Instead of enjoying their retirement, her parents now faced some health issues. Six months ago her dad had bypass surgery, and was only now getting back to his normal self, although her mother said his appetite was still poor.

"My little darlings. I've missed you so much." Louise gave them big kisses, and then crossed the room to kiss Jennie's cheek, her gaze settling on the bandage at her forehead. "Thank heavens you're all right," she exclaimed. "What a frightening accident."

Jennie's father elbowed in and bent to kiss her other cheek, then walked over to shake Nick's hand. "You must be the one who called us. I'm John Howard and this is my wife, Louise. We're very grateful to you."

"Nick Ryan," he said, "and it was the least I could do." He shook both their hands, looking slightly uncomfortable. "The accident was my fault. I was chasing after a puppy, worried that it might get hit by a car. It ran in front of Jennie's SUV. She swerved and lost control. Now she's here instead of home with the two of you."

Jennie appreciated his integrity, but enough was enough. She got to her feet, feeling just a little wobbly. "It wasn't your fault. It was an accident." Tears she blamed on the pain pills pricked her eyes. "Nick's been great," she told her parents. "But enough with the guilt."

Turning away from his puzzled gaze, she put an arm around her mother's back. "It's so good to see you. I'm feeling rather weepy."

"That's nothing to be ashamed of," Louise said. "It's perfectly natural under the circumstance."

Nick picked up his coat. "I'll run down and get your bag. It's in my car."

"Want me to come with you?" her dad asked.

"No, stay here. It'll just take me a sec."

When he left the room, her mother turned to her and raised an eyebrow. "Nice looking man. What does he do?"

"He's a chef."

"Hmmm." She sat down and cradled Brooke in her arms, giving her grandbaby the love and attention she needed and deserved. "I've missed my little bumpkins. I can't wait to have you all home with me." She looked at Jennie, over Brooke's head. "Your dad and I decided to stay overnight. We hate driving late, especially with the snow and traffic so bad."

"Really? It's only a half hour's drive. Wouldn't it be better to take the girls and I'll join you in the morning?"

"That's what I told your mother," her dad said. "But she won't listen."

Louise shook her head, an obstinate look on her face. "Friday night before Christmas? No thank you. Especially with the snow and all. The 95 is a death trap at the best of times."

"Your mother is becoming a nervous wreck," her dad complained. "I told her to stop watching the news."

"And so I should," her mom said defensively. "Can't even go to a movie theater anymore without the threat of getting shot."

"Louise. Don't go on like this in front of the children." Her dad spoke quietly, and took Katie into his arms. She hugged him tight and then peeked out at her Nana.

"What's wrong with the movies?" she asked. "Mom took us to see Frozen."

"I love Frozen!" Brooke said, jumping off Nana's lap.

"And she said we could go to Disney on Ice." Katie turned toward Jennie to make sure the plan hadn't changed. "Didn't you, Mom?"

"Yes," she answered, smiling in spite of the pain. "We will. I promise."

"You will have a wonderful Christmas," Louise said, tilting her small upturned nose in the air. "And your cousins are coming, and Aunt Christy and Uncle Matt."

"Yeah!" Brooke clapped her hands. "I love Jed and Jake. Even when they pull my pigtail."

Louise smiled, and patted her head. "We won't let them do that. But they are very active boys."

John spoke up. "Your mom packed us a light bag. We'll take the girls and stay at a hotel for tonight and in the morning you can see to your car, and then join us."

Jennie's heart sank. So much for nurturing. She longed to be in their familiar house, lying on a sofa next to the fire. Her mother fussing over her and the kids. But it was not to be. She still needed to deal with the insurance company, the police report, renting a car, finish her holiday shopping, and pretend to be happy for her children's sake. This was the first Christmas without Daniel. How could she pretend it was a joyful time, when a vital part of her was still dead inside?

Nick returned with her bag, and she was almost happy to see him.

He handed the large bag on wheels to her father. "If you want dinner before you head back into Philly come to Nick's Bar and Bistro. On Main Street, the town center. Dinner will be on me."

"They're staying here for the night," Jennie told him. "Do you know a hotel nearby?"

"Why sure. There's an Inn—the only Inn in town. At the end of Main Street. It's never full, not even this time of year."

"Sounds good," her mother said. "But I think we'll pass on dinner. Just grab something here so we can spend more time with Jennie." She took her daughter's chin into her hand and studied her face. "What a terrible start to this holiday. And you look so beaten up and exhausted. You need to rest. Stay an extra night, take care of yourself and the car." She glanced at her husband. "Right hon? We don't mind having the children to ourselves. We get so little time with them."

"Whatever Jennie wants is fine by me." John gave her a sympathetic look. "You do look like you've been through a wringer. It's an emotional time for everyone." His kindly eyes swept to his grandchildren. "It's going to be rough on you all."

"I might be able to help speed things up with the car," Nick said, stuffing his hands in his jean pockets. "I know the mechanic. He probably doesn't work weekends, but I could give him a call and see."

"That's not necessary. I'll deal with all this tomorrow." Jennie grimaced, feeling herself sinking a little lower with every breath. "You've been too kind already. Please feel free to go to work. We appreciate everything you've done."

Her mother looked at Nick, then back at her. "Yes. You *have* taken good care of our daughter and girls. Thank you." She reached out a hand and put it on his arm. "Now help me convince my daughter that she doesn't have to do everything herself. She's very stubborn and independent."

"Mom. I have to be. You know that."

The words hung in the air, and her mother's face changed. She nodded and her hazel eyes grew misty. "I know you do. I wish it were different, that's all."

"It's all right, Mom. When I get to your place, you can make all the decisions, and I'll sit back and rest. The car can wait until after the holiday. I need family time," Jennie said, feeling fragile and weak, and hating herself for it. "I haven't seen you since summer, and I want to spend time with Christy and the boys." Her older sister was married to a dentist and had two sons, Jed and Jake, ten and twelve.

"You will," Louise answered. "They're coming around noon on Christmas day, but I expect you'll see them before that." She flashed a worried look at her daughter. "I'm just concerned that you've worn yourself out. The holiday season can do that to anyone, and as a single parent? Well, all I'm saying is that you could probably use a night or two on your own. Just rest and concentrate on getting well."

"I'm okay, Mom. Nothing a night's sleep won't fix."

"Sweetheart, you've been stressed to the max. It's been a terrible year."

"Of course it has. Daniel..." she glanced at her daughters and didn't finish the sentence. Stressed didn't quite cover it. "I want to go home and be with all of you."

"Of course you do," John said, giving his wife a pointed look. He turned to Nick. "Thanks again for taking care of our three girls. You better run off to your restaurant. It's already after six. People will want their chef."

"I'm on my way." Nick nodded at Jennie. "I feel like you got a bad impression of Heaven. I'd love to change your mind." He ruffled Brooke's hair. "I understand that you want to be with your kids, Jennie." His compassionate gaze encompassed them all. "If you decide to wait for the car, there's a lot for the girls to enjoy too. We have an outdoor skating pond, an ice rink, perfect hills for tobogganing, even a horse and carriage ride through the park." He shrugged. "We also have a mall. It's not big, but for last minute presents it's enough."

"Can we, Mom?" Brooke asked. "I want to slide down hills and make a snowman."

Jennie gathered the frayed edges of her temper at the hope shining in her daughter's eyes. "I don't know, hon," Jennie answered. "It makes more sense for me to leave the car here and deal with it next week, after the holidays."

Nick stopped at the doorway. "If I get a vote, I'd like you to stay." Without waiting for a reply he walked away, his solid footsteps echoing down the hall.

"I want to go for a ride in the carriage," Katie said.

"We'll see." Jennie shot her mother a look. "How could you?"

"I wasn't being pushy. I just see that you're on the verge of collapse." Her expression softened. "I miss him too. We all do. We know this is a very difficult time for you."

"What are you talking about?" Katie eyed them both. "Dad?" Her face crumpled. "Why isn't he here? This place is called Heaven. Stupid name, anyway." She burst into tears, and her Papa folded her in his arms.

"There, there, Katie, my girl. It's okay to cry." John gave his wife a look. "Why don't we take the girls to the cafeteria and get them a bite to eat?" He glanced at Brooke who was clinging to her mother. "You guys hungry?"

A nurse came around the corner. "Your room is ready. Why don't your visitors come up to room 302 in about twenty minutes, once we have you settled?"

John put his hand on Katie's shoulder and held the other hand out to Brooke. "Yes, we'll grab dinner and see you in half an hour," he said, leading her daughters away. "Come, Louise."

Louise bent and kissed Jennie on the forehead. "Just think about it, will you? You need to take care of yourself so that you'll be strong enough for the girls." Then she followed her husband and grandkids from the room.

Jennie watched them leave, but her mind was on Nick and his last words. He wanted her to stay. Why did that give her a warm, fuzzy feeling, and make her want to smile? Not that she would let her mother know that. It would be her own little secret, and one she would hold dear.

CHAPTER THREE

Nick rushed down the brightly lit corridor of Heaven's only hospital as fast as his legs could carry him. "I would like you to stay." His words mocked him every step of the way. What an idiot! She was either divorced or a widow, for heaven's sake. She probably wanted a husband, and if she didn't, her mother certainly did. It would only be a matter of time before that idea was firmly implanted into Jennie's brain, and he didn't want to be around when that happened. She was young, beautiful, with two adorable girls. Of course she would want a husband. He wasn't in the market for a wife.

Idiot! Moron! If he had a brain it must be tucked away in his pants.

He tossed his bulky ski jacket over his shoulders as he exited the building and headed for his Jeep. Earlier this morning he'd made his mainstays, chili, stew and lasagna, but tonight's special was Coq au Vin and it needed some prep time.

As Jennie's father had pointed out, it was after six. The restaurant opened for lunch six days a week, and then again at five. His bartender, Byron, and Ally, his waitress, were taking care of things until he could get there. They were more than capable but still it was his responsibility to make sure things ran smoothly. He took his phone from his jacket pocket and dialed the first number that came up.

"Nick's Bar and Bistro," Ally said cheerfully.

"Hi Ally. How's it going?" He'd already given them an update earlier, after seeing Jennie and her girls off in the ambulance. Ally told him not to worry, that she'd get the salad and bread out to the customers, and offered to chop up the chicken before the place got busy.

"No problem, boss. We only have three tables right now, and I can handle that fine. I'm pushing the stew and chili. So far so good," she said with a nervous giggle. "You on your way?"

"Yup. Will be there in a few minutes. Just wanted to tell you that you're brilliant and beautiful, and I should give you a raise."

"I'll hold you to that." He heard people chatting and laughing, and the sound of Bing Crosby crooning in the background. He imagined the bar was still packed, people enjoying their two for one's, hoping the weather would clear and make the roads safer for their journey home.

"Don't rush," she said. "The streets are bad. How's the woman?"

"She's good. Might have a severe headache, but I don't think it's any worse than that. They have to hold her overnight for observation." He was glad that Jennie hadn't forced the issue of leaving. Maybe he shouldn't have shared his story about his friend's sister, but he didn't want anything bad to happen to the vulnerable mother of two. "As you can imagine, she's not happy about it."

"Don't blame her. Did her parent's get there?"

"Yes. They're nice people."

"Okay," Ally said. "She's in good hands. You've done all that you can."

"For now." Jennie's big green eyes haunted him. "I'll take care of the car in the morning."

"Righteo then. I've got the chicken pieces marinating in the spices and wine."

"Thanks, Ally. Tell Byron to go light on the pours. Don't want anyone getting a DUI tonight, or ending up wrapped around a pole. One accident is enough."

"I'll tell him."

"But will he listen?"

"Of course he will. He wants in my pants," she said with a laugh.

"Yours and everyone else's," Nick answered quickly. "Please tell me he hasn't been there."

"That's for me to know." With that she hung up.

Nick shook his head, figuring she was too smart for Byron. He didn't know squat about her sex life, but she deserved better than to be in one continuous parade of women.

Ally was a bit of a mystery to him, living by herself outside of town. She'd started working for him about this time last year, and he assumed she'd be gone within six months. She was young—only twenty-five—and from Connecticut. He thought a sleepy little town like Heaven would bore her to tears, but that wasn't the case. She loved to hike and take photos of nature which she blew up and framed.

The walls of the restaurant boasted many of her personal favorites. She was good and people offered to buy them, but she was reluctant to sell. Why she chose to work in his restaurant instead of making a name for herself as a photographer was anyone's guess.

Byron had shown up just as he was opening his restaurant two years ago, and Nick had hired him on the spot. Nick didn't think he'd last either, but he was still pouring the best drinks in town, spouting poetry to anyone who would listen, and filling the bar with the happy hour crowd. He changed girlfriends about as often as he did underwear, but if that was his thing, it wasn't up to Nick to judge. As long as he wasn't messing with under-aged girls or Ally he could do whatever and whoever he liked.

Nick pulled into the small parking lot behind his restaurant and sat there for a moment lost in thought. He knew Christmas music played inside, people would be wearing their ugly sweaters and pretending it was the season to be jolly. He knew better. Christmas was probably the unhappiest time of the year. More suicides. Too much spending, too many expectations, and too many disappointments that led to despair. He'd lost his own Grandma on Christmas day—the woman who'd loved and raised him as her own.

He couldn't remember much of his life before moving in with Grandma and Pops, but occasionally he'd have a flashback or two. He remembered a fire. A tree being knocked over. People yelling and fighting, and that's all.

He never saw that house again. His mother visited once in awhile for the first few years, then she disappeared one day and never came back.

It must be hard for Jennie, he thought. He didn't know when she lost her husband, but he was obviously out of the picture. He had seen the sadness in her eyes, and as much as he wished her happiness, he couldn't offer it. He needed to remember that. If she didn't leave right away he would have to tread carefully, and not give her any false hope, like asking her to stay.

Sheesh, Almighty, what had he been thinking? Not clearly, that's for sure. She was pretty, perhaps even beautiful and he loved her gentle smile, the light in her eyes as she looked at her kids. But he wasn't looking for a woman. Not by a long shot, and children? Forget about it. They were like puppies. Cute to look at and fun to be around, but high maintenance. Even a girlfriend stretched his limits.

He stepped out of his car, bracing for the cold, and ran the few steps to the back door. It was unlocked and as he entered his kitchen he felt the world around him right itself. Just the sight of the place was like seeing an old friend. The pots and pans, the spotless counter tops and butcher board, commercial stove and fridge were all a welcome sight. He smelled the basil, bay leaf and thyme, the burgundy wine in the pot of stew. The chili was simmering on the stove, and he knew a fresh loaf of sourdough bread was warming in the oven.

He was home. His grandma had taught him how to cook and had nurtured his curiosity and sense of adventure in the kitchen. What he hadn't learned from her he'd been taught in the best culinary regions in Europe. He'd spent two years apprenticing after graduating from high school, and then had worked in Philadelphia and Manhattan for several years honing his trade.

Ally pushed her way through the swinging doors. "So you finally got here." She smiled and looked at him closely. "What's up? You look different."

"Oh, I just spent the past few minutes down memory lane. No problem. I'm back where I want to be."

"Good! We have a foursome who just walked in and they want your Coq au Vin. I'll get them their salads and bread. Need help with anything else?"

"Nope. You're a sweetheart. I'll get this out to them in about ten minutes."

"Okay, boss. Glad you made it here. I was getting worried about you."

"I'm fine. Hopefully, we'll still get some late shoppers stopping by for a decent meal." He picked up a tasting spoon. "I haven't eaten since noon. What do you recommend?"

"People are raving about your stew. But you already know that."

"Music to my ears."

Nick chowed down on a cup of stew, then got to work. He was happiest in the kitchen and soon he was singing along to the damn holiday music that Ally insisted the customers wanted to hear.

The last thing he wanted was to be a Scrooge, so he tucked away his dislike of Christmas into a deeper corner of his mind, and set out to create mouth-watering chicken swimming in a velvety wine sauce savored with fresh herbs and spices.

When it was done, he placed it artfully on four white plates and carried it himself to the waiting couples. He presented the dishes with a flourish and a friendly grin.

"Sorry to keep you waiting, folks. Had a little family emergency." Not his family, but what did it matter? "Desserts will be on the house."

"Well, that's real nice of you," the man said with a surprised look toward his wife. "Everything has been wonderful."

"Your bread is fabulous." She buttered a corner piece. "Is it from a local bakery?"

"No. It's baked here. A family recipe that my grandma taught me."

"Well, tell her it's the best bread I've ever had."

"I'd like to, ma'am, but she's in a different heaven." He smiled and returned to the sanctuary of his kitchen, where he sat on a stool and slowly ate the crust of the loaf. His thoughts flew to Jennie. This would be a perfect place for her and the children. Close to her parents, but just far enough away that she could have a life of her own. It was safe and friendly, and had a hellova restaurant too.

CHAPTER FOUR

The following morning Nick got out of bed, put his slippers on and a long wool bathrobe, and opened the sliding patio door to let Sammy, his Samoyed, out for his morning pee. Sammy blended in with the snow. Before he knew what was happening a little black and white floppy-eared pup squeezed through his legs and ran out too.

Nick groaned and muttered a curse. He hadn't even had his coffee yet. And he'd completely forgotten about the puppy he'd brought home. He ran to get some doggy treats, then stepped out in the freezing cold to lure the excited pup in. The pup was chasing the older dog, jumping through the snow with unabashed delight and leaving yellow puddles of snow in his wake.

"Come here. Yeah, you." Nick held out a biscuit to the young dog, but Sammy was too quick on the uptake and nipped it out of his hand. Then he jumped up, putting his wet paws on Nick's chest.

"Down, boy." He gave his pet an affectionate hug before pushing him away and feeding him another biscuit. "We've got to get this trouble maker into the house," he said to Sammy, as he tried sneaking up on the pup, who eyed him warily, and then as he drew near, he yipped and ran around in circles, excited to start the chase again.

Nick was no longer in the mood. "Suit yourself, you little shit. I'm having my coffee and you can stay out here, or come in. Your choice." He climbed the three steps to his porch and opened the door for Sammy, who followed him obediently.

The pup didn't know what was good for him and continued to bark and run around the back yard, spraying everywhere he went.

Nick left him to make his coffee, shower and dress. Ten minutes later he entered the kitchen in a fresh pair of jeans, a checkered flannel shirt, and a cream-colored knit sweater.

He poured his coffee, wondering how Jennie was feeling this morning. A bit bruised, he'd expect. Probably restless too. She must have been looking forward to spending the holidays with her parents. They looked like good people who loved her and the girls very much. Whatever had happened to her husband, well, it was sad and must still hurt a lot.

Nick heard a scratch at the patio door and looked over to see the puppy shivering on the porch with a sappy look on his face. Grabbing a handful of treats, Nick opened the door, bent down and handfed the mutt, then stepped back, enticing the pup forward. Once he was safely in, Nick slid the glass door closed. "Gotchya."

Next he dialed the hospital, his shoulders tense. Jennie had told him that she was fine, but he couldn't help feeling responsible for the accident.

When he was put through to Jennie's room and heard her voice, he smiled. "Good morning, Jennie. It's Nick. How're you feeling today?" Dumb question. She probably hurt like hell and lying there in a hospital bed, he doubted that she slept much at all. He hadn't. His mind couldn't shut down—visual images of the car sliding on the ice and slamming into that damn tree, the kids in the back screaming. The minute it took him to reach the car and get the kids out had seemed like forever. He'd opened her door next and found her out cold, her forehead bleeding. No darn wonder he'd had nightmares.

"Okay," she said. "But I don't want to be here."

"I get it. You're supposed to be at your parent's home right now, enjoying breakfast with them. Instead you're stuck alone in a hospital bed." He pushed his coffee to the side. "That sucks."

"Yeah, that about sums it up," she answered with a soft sigh. "It could be a lot worse. At least the kids weren't hurt."

"Exactly." He wanted to make it up to her, but wasn't sure how. Then inspiration hit. "I was thinking of calling your parents at the Inn and inviting them and the girls to the best waffles in town. Do you think they'd like that?"

"I suppose so. Kids love the Waffle House near us in Norfolk. At your restaurant?"

"No, I'll make blueberry waffles here. They can play with the puppy." The little dog's ears lifted. "They would enjoy that, and so would he."

"You're going to cook my parents and kids breakfast?" she asked, her voice breaking.

33

"I was thinking that might be a good idea." He hesitated, wondering why she sounded upset. Was it too forward of a move? "They're stuck at the Inn and trust me, their food is nowhere as good as mine."

She sniffed. "That's nice of you, but, but…"

"But what?" He kept his voice gentle, not sure why she was crying. He was trying to do something nice. The puppy cocked his head as if he were listening.

"But I want to come!" she cried, her voice catching. "That sounds like fun. And I'm stuck here. I just wanted to go home. I hate Christmas, especially this year."

Nick totally understood that sentiment. "Jennie, I'm sorry. I put you in the hospital and this is my fault. Hey, your holiday might be off to a rocky start, but you'll still have a wonderful Christmas with your family. You should be out of the hospital later this morning. You can have breakfast too."

"No, I can't. The doctor won't be making his rounds until later, and I'm not cleared to leave until he sees me. Then there's the paperwork. The nurse said it would probably be noon." She sniffed again and her genuine distress made Nick's heart ache. "I'm sorry, but I feel so weepy. Probably the after effects of the accident and the pills they gave me to sleep."

"You're probably right." Nick figured she had plenty of reason to cry. "So I won't invite your family for breakfast. Instead, how about you all join me at the restaurant for lunch? Nick's Bar and Bistro. On Main Street. We're open from noon until two-thirty each day, then reopen at five."

"You don't have to do that," she said. "We'll grab a bite on our way out of town. I just want to get out of here." Her voice broke again. "I feel so lonely." She was silent for a few seconds then added in a whisper, "This is my first Christmas without my husband. He died in January."

He heard her crying, and his heart turned over. He hated a woman's tears, or anyone hurting. Not that he remembered much about his mother, but he'd never forget the terrible sobs coming from the thin wall separating his room from hers. She was always unhappy, and the men that came by to see her made it so much worse—leaving her totally destroyed, unable to get out of bed, to make his breakfast, to care for him. There had been times when he'd hated her, but he loved her too. "That must be really hard, Jennie. I'm so sorry to hear that."

"Thanks."

She sounded like she was hanging on by a thread, and he wanted so much to see her smile and make her happy again. If only for a moment. Loneliness he understood. He'd spent most of his life feeling like an outsider, someone who breathed the same air, but didn't quite fit in.

"Please don't rush to leave," he said. "We normally close at two-thirty, but I could make an exception today and close early. It's a beautiful day outside, and I'd like to take the girls to the pond for a little ice skating after lunch. I know they'd love it, and they rent skates there, so that wouldn't be a problem. There are benches where you and your parents could sit and watch, and they sell cocoa and coffee. Delicious donuts as well."

"That does sound nice," she said in a husky voice, her tears slowing. "You don't need to go to this trouble for us."

"But I want to," he insisted. "I want to make it up to you and the girls. We could all go for a drive after skating too. I want you to see Heaven the way I do."

"Why are you being so kind?"

"Because…" He had no idea. "Because I want to start your holiday off by doing something fun. Forget this nasty accident and your car, and all the bad things that have happened recently, and just be happy for one afternoon. Just one. Okay?"

She waited so long he worried there was a bad connection, but then she said, "Okay. That's a deal." It sounded like she might be smiling, which made him feel better, too. "One day without looking back. Just moving forward. I like that. One day at a time," she added slowly. "It could be my new mantra."

"It's a good one." He didn't want to say good-bye. Talking to her was comfortable, as if he'd known her his entire life instead of less than twenty-four hours. "I'll check on your car before I go to work. You want me to come around and check on you as well?"

She laughed, which made his heart jump. "No. My parents and kids will be here soon. We'll come for lunch as soon as they let me get the hell out of here." Jennie lowered her voice. "Oops. Here comes someone with my breakfast tray. I hope it's not waffles. I would rather taste yours." With that he heard a click and knew she'd hung up.

He stood there holding the phone for several seconds, wondering what had made him feel so good. Her laugh, the teasing remark about the waffles, the thought of her staying for an afternoon of fun? Or all of the above?

Maybe it was time for him to get a girlfriend of his own. If the thought of being with this woman and her family for just a few hours could lift his spirits then perhaps this quiet lifestyle needed shaking up. "No man is an island," he told the inquisitive puppy at his feet. "A little female company could be a whole lot more entertaining than coming home to the likes of you every night."

The puppy yapped and danced around the table.

"Don't think you're staying," Nick said, heading to the kitchen to fry up some bacon and eggs. As he ate, he decided to make up some posters to put around town. The pup had to belong to someone, and he didn't need two free loaders taking up his space. Sammy sprawled out in front of the fireplace. The puppy had managed to jump on the sofa and was now comfortably chewing on his throw pillow.

He stuck the dishes in the dishwasher, then used his digital camera and took some photos of the sleeping dog—all innocent and cute—under the headline LOST DOG, he added his contact information and the name of his restaurant where he could be reached. Twenty should be enough, he figured.

Putting on his boots and coat, he considered going to the hospital to surprise Jennie, but she'd have her kids and parents there. If she was alone? Yeah, different story. Now he had to spend the next few hours hoping she'd come to the restaurant. If not for his fabulous lunch and company, then at least for news about the car.

When he arrived at the gas station Nick spotted the SUV inside the body shop. He walked right in, his gut knotting at the messed up front end. "Hi, Jack," he nodded to the mechanic that enjoyed happy hour on Friday nights at his bar. "So, what do you think?"

"Looks like you hit a tree," Jack drawled, and shook his head. Dressed in gray denim coveralls and black work boots, the middle-aged man had a stubbly white beard and a knit cap over his graying hair.

"Not me. Car belongs to a woman by the name of Jennie Braxton. She's on her way to Philly. I was chasing some damn dog and to avoid the pup she skidded into the tree. Saw the whole damn thing." Nick rubbed his jaw. "She's got two little girls too. Scary as shit."

"Good thing nobody got hurt," Jack said. "So where's the woman now?"

"Had to be checked out at the hospital. She should be here soon." Nick walked around the car, feeling sick to his stomach. "How much damage?"

"It'll need a new window, paint, body work." He wiped his hands on his back pockets. "The suspension needs fixing, and the steering post's been damaged."

"Crap. Is there any good news?" Nick looked at the front end, grateful that it had somehow saved Jennie's life. "Can't believe the airbags didn't deploy."

"Neither can I." Jack shrugged. "She'll need those checked out too."

"How long before it's ready?"

"A good week to ten days, due to the holiday, and ordering parts. But I can't start until the insurance adjustor comes out."

Not the best news, Nick thought. But it would keep Jennie in town an extra day or two. And she'd definitely be coming back to Heaven for her fixed car.

He wouldn't mind that a bit. Matter of fact, he looked forward to telling her the sorry news, and how he planned to make it up to her.

"Thanks. We'll be in touch."

Nick found himself singing along to Jingle Bell Rock on his radio station during the short drive to work. Remembering Jennie's shy confession that she'd rather eat his waffles and promise to have fun, lifted his spirits. So much in fact that he almost enjoyed the cheery music.

As he entered the back door of the restaurant, Nick prepped his menu for the day. A huge pot of beef and barley soup, and another of Boston Clam Chowder. While that simmered on the stove, he rolled out some pastries to make quiche. Two Quiche Lorraine's went into the oven, followed by another two with crab and asparagus. As they baked he started on a dozen single-sized portion chicken pot pies.

After that, he poured himself a half glass of Pinot Grigio and sat down to wait.

CHAPTER FIVE

By the time Jennie's parents came to get her at the hospital it was just before noon. She'd showered, then dressed in her favorite sage-colored sweater and jeans. Nick's thoughtfulness in bringing her bag allowed her to have her own things, and clean clothes. The bloodstained top she'd worn in the car could be tossed for all she cared. A reminder that she didn't need. This family had already had enough tragedy this year. "What took you so long?" she asked, giving her girls big hugs, and holding them a little longer than usual. "Hungry? Nick called earlier." She ignored her mom's sharp look of interest and continued in a breezy manner. "He invited us to lunch and a nice afternoon skating." Jennie glanced at her daughter's hopeful expression, and met her father's eyes. "We don't have to do that, of course. We could just go see about the car. I got a hold of my insurance company this morning, and they're attempting to find an adjustor who'll come out here today. No promises however." She shrugged. "The good news is that my insurance covers a rental car. So I'm all set there."

Her dad sat at the edge of the bed, looking tired. "Whatever you want to do is fine by me."

He looked so frail sitting there, that she felt guilty dragging him away from the comfort of his home to rescue her and the girls. He probably hadn't slept very well sharing a room with two energetic kids.

"Let's skip it," she decided, wanting to get him home where he could rest. "I'll just call Nick or we can drop in and tell him we can't stay. No big deal. We have to come back after the holidays to pick up the car anyway. We can do it then."

"I want to go skating," Katie pouted. "Who cares about the stupid car?"

"I want to see the puppy again," Brooke said. "If he doesn't want to keep him and he doesn't belong to anyone, can we take him home with us?"

"Now isn't the best time, Brooke. We'd have to keep him at Nana's for a week, and he probably isn't house trained yet. Then we'd have to cage him in the car on the return trip. I'd like to wait and get a dog when we have our new home."

"I wish we could have the pup from yesterday," Brooke said sadly. "I've already named him Spot. He was so cute and cuddly."

"That's a dorky name," Katie told her and made a face. "Spot? Don't be a silly ninny."

"Girls, behave. You're wearing Papa out. Me too." She helped her dad up, and kissed his cheek. "I bet you didn't sleep a wink all night. The girls have been so excited about seeing you both."

"No, they fell asleep before nine, but that little one sure can snore." He chuckled. "Even louder than me."

She grabbed her bag on wheels and followed her parents and the children to the elevator and the car. "How was the Inn? Nice?"

"It was lovely," her mother said. "English Tudor in style. The rooms were large and roomy, with two King sized beds. Nice big flat screen TV, comfy bedding and a great shower. Decent breakfast too."

"Oh, that's good to hear. Nick wanted to invite you all over for waffles, but I told him that wasn't necessary. He's already done so much for us. Got the car towed to the station, gave the police a preliminary report. He doesn't need to cook breakfast for my family too." She blushed, remembering how emotional she'd gotten over the phone with him earlier.

"He's a very pleasant and thoughtful man," her mother said.

"Feels guilty for putting you in the hospital, more likely," her dad replied. "Can't blame him. When I think what could have happened to the three of you…"

"It really wasn't his fault," she broke in, not wanting to even consider another outcome. "He was trying to catch the dog, and I would have run the little guy over if I hadn't seen him just in time. The car slid on some ice and smacked into that tree. Could have happened even without him and the dog."

When they reached her father's car, she put the girl's in the booster seats in the back. She had bought them for her parents a few years back. Then she slid in between the two seats, and was glad that she had small hips because it was a narrow fit.

"Dad, if you don't mind, just pull up in front of Nick's restaurant and I'll pop in and make our excuses. He told me we'd see it. Nick's Bistro on Main Street."

She knew he'd be disappointed. For some reason he seemed determined to want to make her happy. As if an afternoon skating could do that.

Her happiness had died along with her husband and it would be a long time before she'd feel anything close to that again. She wasn't ready to let go off her grief, or to let his memory slip away. She reminded herself everyday of how much she'd loved him, and how much she missed him. Happiness had no place in her life right now. So Nick could just find some other poor dog, or person in distress to lavish his attention on.

When they got to Main Street, they discovered there was no parking. It was a quaint cobblestone street and they had to park in a lot a block away. "You can all wait here, if you like. No point in all of us getting out."

Her mother glanced in the back at the girls. "You girls want a quick bite to eat? We had breakfast several hours ago."

"I do. I do," Brooke said, and Katie nodded her head.

"Guess, I wouldn't mind something too." Her dad found a parking spot, and they all piled out of the car while he put a couple of quarters into a machine. The children ran ahead, slipping and sliding along the sidewalk, while Jennie and her mother glanced into store windows.

It was a lovely day. The sun was shining and snow glistened on the tree-lined street. Jennie could see the store front windows and pretty Evergreen trees twinkled with fairy lights, even this early in the day. As they walked under an awning, light snow fine as gossamer or cotton candy sprinkled down upon them. The girls laughed and tried to catch a drop in their hands but it was gone before they could grasp it.

Seeing this magical street—like something out of a movie—made her smile. Her tension melted just like the snow, and for the first time in almost a year she felt herself relax. She lifted her head.

"Heaven, Daniel?" she asked silently. "Is this what it's like? Was it you watching over us? I miss you."

"Mom?" Brooke ran up to her and pulled at her hand, she was still missing a mitten. "What are you doing?"

"Nothing, honey. Just looking at the fluffy snowflakes falling off the roofs," she told them. "And look at these streetlamps. I don't think I've ever seen lamps like these before. They even have candy cane stripes." She pulled out her i-Phone and took a selfie with the girls. With a cracked face, she wasn't sure if it would come out, and she didn't really care. It amused the girls and that alone was worth the second it took.

Her mother had linked arms with her dad and they were walking down the middle of the street, shoulders bumping, looking as much in love as when they'd first met forty years ago.

"Mom? If we have to move, why don't we get a house here?" Brooke's voice held that little girl quality that Katie had outgrown. "I like this place, but I'm gonna miss our house and the swings in the backyard. And the rabbits." She skipped along beside her. "Will there be rabbits at Nana's?"

"Not this time of the year. But maybe we'll see deer."

"A reindeer?" she asked.

"No. Just the regular variety." On the other side of the road she saw a bright sign that caught her eye. Nick's Bar and Bistro. "There it is." She called out to her parents. "Nick's."

When they stood outside the cafe she peered into the window and noticed the red and white tablecloths, candles on each table, and a fireplace that looked warm and inviting. "You're sure you have time for lunch? I know you want to get home before the traffic picks up."

"We still have plenty of time. Is that adjustor fellow going to call your cell if he can get here today?"

"That's the plan. If I don't hear from him, I'll call the office again after we've had lunch." She pushed open the door and held it for her parents and her kids to enter.

A guy behind the bar shouted out a friendly greeting. "Welcome to Nick's!"

The waitress, a young woman with short, spiky dark hair and a wide smile, came over with some menus in hand. "You must be Jennie, and these are your kids, and the grandparents. I'm sorry to hear about your accident and hope you're all right?"

Jennie answered with surprise. "We're all fine, thank you."

The waitress turned to her parents. "Not exactly the way you hoped your visit would start."

"No, but it could have been worse," Louise said, smiling politely.

"Well, I'm Ally, your server. Nick's been expecting you and he asked me to take very good care of you. He also said that lunch is on the house—and if you don't mind me making a suggestion, Nick makes an excellent quiche. Crab and asparagus is my favorite. His soups are fabulous too."

"It all sounds good." Jennie smiled at the young cheerful woman with the flashing brown eyes and a flowered tattoo peeking out of her blouse. "This will be a pleasant way to spend an hour."

"Here. Let me take your coats. We just hang them on the hooks."

"We can do that," Jennie said, not willing to be treated like royalty. "Where would you like us to sit?"

"Take any seat that you want. The booths might be a bit small but one of the round tables will sit six comfortably."

Glancing around the room, Jennie noticed the dozen or so wooden tables, half of them empty. She chose the one nearest the fire, and the girls began to peel off their coats and gloves and goofy hats. A row of hooks near the door was used to hang jackets, so she hung up the girls' and her own. Her mother and dad added theirs and then took the chairs with their backs to the fire.

"The menu is here on the wall." The bartender's voice carried from his spot behind the bar. "It changes daily." He had a nice face, attractive features, with light brown wavy hair that was thick and glossy. Jennie imagined a lot of young woman would consider him hot. Matter of fact, there was a table of three pretty teenagers giggling in the corner, sneaking peaks in his direction.

"I'll let Nick know you're here," the waitress said. "Then I'll be back for your order."

Jennie was reading the chalk menu when the swinging door to the kitchen opened up and Nick came out, making his way to their table.

Jennie felt her heart skip a beat, and wondered why in the world it was fluttering. Louise waved to him, and he came up and kissed her hand.

"Oh my," she said, batting her eyes at him. "You're making me blush."

His laugh was charming. "Glad you came. I was afraid that you might sneak out of town and not let me at least offer you a meal for your troubles."

Her dad folded a napkin on the table top. "Kids haven't had anything since an early breakfast. Jennie still has some business to do this afternoon, so we were happy to take you up on your offer."

Jennie stood next to Nick, admiring his easy manner. Relaxed, and in his element. He turned his attention to her. "How are you doing?"

"Better." She tucked a strand of hair behind her ear, oddly nervous. "Thanks."

"That's good." He pulled out her chair and she slid in. Her knees felt a little wobbly.

"Good. I went to the gas station this morning and got some information on your car." He put his hand on Jennie's shoulder and looked into her face. "Want the good news now, and the bad after lunch?"

She made a face. "How bad?"

"Bad enough."

"Okay. Guess I better eat first." Her eyes met his warm brown ones with a spark of hope. Good news was better than bad, any day of the week. "I'll take the good news though."

"You may get to stay another night," he said, his dark brows lifted like a game show host.

She laughed and put her hand over her mouth. The last thing she wanted was to stay. "That's supposed to be the good news?"

"Yeah," he said with a nod. "We can do the horse and carriage thing. It'll be fun, and I think you could use some of that."

Jennie shook her head, not buying into that idea. "So, why do I "get" to stay overnight? There is no way my car is going to be fixed anytime soon so once the insurance adjustor shows up, I'm free to leave."

"True," he readily agreed. "It's going to take at least a week. There's also a problem with the suspension and steering post."

"That's the good news or the bad?" Jennie kept her smile in place but her stomach was churning. She couldn't really afford anymore big bills now. Not before Christmas, and certainly not until after her house was sold.

"The bad. Sorry, it kind of slipped out." He looked at her seriously. "Please don't worry about it. The accident was my fault and I'll cover the costs."

"That's not necessary," her father pointed out. "Her insurance will take care of it."

"Well, any out of pocket costs," Nick amended. "I insist. And that includes you renting a car."

"That's covered by my insurance too." Jennie sat back and peered up at him. "So let's have lunch then I can get my rented car and leave later today."

Her mom smiled at Nick. "So, what do you suggest?"

"Soup's good. Beef and barley or clam chowder, and Ally probably mentioned my quiche. It's a big seller. But I also have chili and lasagna."

"I want chili," Katie told Nick.

"Not me," said Brooke. "I want a grilled cheese sandwich, or chicken fingers."

"That's not on the menu, Brooke, but maybe you could ask the chef." Smiling, Jennie glanced up at him, and her heart did a little pitter-patter. What the heck? Was she flirting?

"Anything for this little princess," Nick said, giving Brooke a wink.

"I'm not a princess," Brooke replied. "I'm a cookie monster. Cookie, cookie," she said pretending to stuff her mouth.

Ally brought iced water to the table and crayons and Christmas scenes for the girls to color. They settled down, content to wait for their lunch.

Her dad ordered the barley soup and Quiche Lorraine, while Jennie and her mom decided on crab quiche and iced tea.

She sipped her tea, and the knots in her shoulders relaxed a little. Her mother was coloring with the girls, her dad was enjoying his soup, and she had a moment to simply appreciate the fact that they were alive, and here.

Together in a place that was Heaven on earth. The thought actually made her smile.

The bistro had a warm, homey feeling to the decor. The walls were a wood grain on the bottom, and had an attractive wallpaper motif on the top. Terrific pictures of wildlife were framed and hung around the room. A night or two in this adorable town might actually take all her stress away. It was definitely therapeutic.

Her mom patted her hand. "Things have gotten awfully complicated, haven't they honey?"

Jennie nodded, unable to speak after seeing the compassion in her mother's eyes.

"It's all going to work out fine. I have a good feeling."

"What do you mean? This is an extra expense that I certainly don't need."

"That's true, but I believe things happen for a reason. And I'm sorry, but it brought you here. I think it's all part of the divine plan."

"Divine plan, be damned," John muttered, rubbing his chest. "What a cockabilly idea. It's a nuisance, but these things happen and we just have to deal with them."

The girls looked up from their coloring. "What's cockabilly, Papa?"

Jennie pulled her gaze from her dad and laughed softly. "It means silly, and you girls know how to be silly, don't you?"

She tickled them both and made them giggle. But while she waited for lunch, she thought about what her mother said. Had there been a reason for her to turn off the highway when she did, and end up in Heaven? Had Daniel been in on this scheme? The idea lightened her heart. Or was her dad right, and these things, like his health issues, just had to be dealt with?

The decision to stay or to go would be made for her. If the adjustor got here this afternoon she'd be free to leave. Didn't mean she couldn't come back after the holiday and spend a night or two. Get to know the town a little better. Nick too.

She had options. The door to Heaven was open.

CHAPTER SIX

Nick took out a chicken breast, pounded it with his mallet, then chopped it into finger-like slices. He dipped the chicken strips into an egg mixture, then breadcrumbs and sautéed them over the grill. While they were cooking, he quickly grilled a cheese sandwich, and sliced a banana and strawberries on a plate. When the chicken fingers were a nice golden brown, he took them off the grill, and put them on the plate, along with the half sandwich. Brooke may only be five, but his attention to detail remained the same as if she were fifty-five.

Pleased with the artful display, he delivered the meal himself. The fact he'd get another chance to converse and look at Jennie was an additional bonus. Brooke grinned up at him when she saw her lunch plate. "That's for me?"

"It is. Special compliments of the chef."

She blinked, her eyes big and round. "Are you the chef?"

"I am."

"Then where's your hat?" She pointed to his head. "You should wear one of those big floppy white hats."

"Now, that's a good question." He glanced at Jennie, who was playing with her food and smiling at the conversation.

"If you don't have one," Brooke said, "you could wear mine. It's a piggy hat."

"A piggy hat?" Nick nodded, fighting back a smile. "Wow. That sounds really nice, but I'm not sure that my big head would fit into a little girl's piggy hat."

She giggled. "Want to try? It's on the hook over there," she pointed, "with my pink coat."

Nick glanced where the little girl pointed, then his eyes met Jennie's. He quirked his brow. "Um. Do I have to?"

"Of course not. But you would win her heart forever." Her eyes sparkled. "Not necessary, trust me. It was enough that you made her a special meal."

"Can I have a sliced banana and strawberries, too?" Katie asked. "I'm almost done with my chili."

"Now, Katie. Nick's busy, don't bother him," Louise said and patted her hand. "If you ask nicely, I'm sure Brooke will share hers."

Brooke nodded. "Here you go, Katie." She picked up a couple of slices and put them on her sister's bread plate. "You can have those."

Jennie looked at her children with maternal pride. "They're very good at sharing." She turned her attention back on him, probably wondering why he was still hanging around with nothing better to do. "The quiche is fabulous, by the way. Where did you learn to cook?"

"My grandma mostly. She raised me, and we spent a lot of time in the kitchen together." He rubbed his jaw, still defensive about his love for his grandma and cooking—a hangover from his youth. "After she passed away, I started working at one of the local chain restaurants on weekends and for the summers. Started off as a busboy, then a waiter, and graduated to a short order cook. Stayed there for a few years, until I was twenty-three. Went to Europe for a couple of years."

"Cool," Jennie said, her posture relaxed. Interested. "I've never spent any real time in Europe. Used to fly there when I worked for the airlines before the kids came along." She smiled. "Always wanted to go back to some of my favorite cities and explore them more."

She did have that flight attendant look about her. Tall, attractive, put together. But a lot friendlier than most of them. "I apprenticed under some of the best chefs in the big cities around Europe. Paris. Rome. Malaga."

"Lovely," Louise said, her hand on her husband's arm. "The two of us plan to take a trip to Europe next year, God willing. One of those land tours." She smiled. "Did you visit the museums, or were you too busy for that?"

"I took in a few, after all art and food go hand in hand. Must admit, I was having the time of my life," he told them. "You two should go. It's a great experience."

"We will," John said. "Had a health scare this past year, but that's not going to keep me grounded. I promised Louise we'd travel once we retired, and I aim to keep my promise."

"When you're up to it," Louise said with a loving smile.

Nick turned back to Jennie. "Truthfully, I was more interested in the art of food than museums. I learned a few tricks of the trade and some management skills.

Enough for me to open and run this place here." He glanced around at his bistro with pride. "It's not much, but I like it."

"You should," Jennie said, nodding with approval. "Your food is hearty and the décor rustic. The fireplace creates the perfect ambience." She looked like she wanted to say more, but was hesitant.

Not so with her mother. Louise had no trouble speaking up. "What an interesting life you've led, Nick. You say your grandparents raised you? How did that happen, if you don't mind me asking?"

He did mind, but now that the question was on the table he'd answer it the best way he could. He met her eyes, then Jennie's, and lastly, John's. For some reason, he wanted the man's approval.

With a slight shrug of his shoulder, he turned his palms up. "Not much to say. My mother knew she couldn't take care of me, so she left me with her parents. I never saw her again after I was six. Never knew my dad." He looked down at the table, then lifted his head again. "Most people in this neck of the woods know I was raised by my grandparents. Folks don't understand why I ever came back."

"Oh!" Jennie's eyes were wide and full of sympathy, something he hated. No one needed to feel sorry for him. He had been brought up with all the love in the world. "Why *did* you return? I would think you'd have stayed in Europe. It sounds so romantic and exciting."

"It is and I was tempted." He tucked his hands behind his back. "But then my grandpa needed someone to take care of him, so I came home. It was a good decision." He paused. "I'd been away long enough."

He saw respect in their eyes and straightened his shoulders. "I'll let you get on with your lunch. If you want dessert, we have a carrot cake or apple pie. Can't go wrong with either."

"I'll have some of that pie," John said. "A scoop of ice cream on the side, if you don't mind."

Nick grinned. "Pie warmed?"

"Is there any other way," John said with a pleased nod. "How about you, girls?" He glanced at both women and the grandkids. "Anyone else want something sweet?"

"Cookies, cookies, cookies," Brooke said, doing the cookie monster routine again.

Nick surprised the little girl by saying, "I'll bring over a plate of Christmas cookies for the table."

"Now you really did win her heart," Jennie said, her big green eyes on him.

He flushed with pleasure. "I also have a special treat that might be more fun than cookies."

"More fun than cookies?" Brooke chimed. "What is it?" She bounced in her seat.

"It's a favorite activity for guests of all ages." He smiled at their mystified expressions and wary faces. "Who likes roasting marshmallows in a campfire?"

"I do," Katie clapped her hands. "Can we, Mom?"

"Yes! Can we?" Brooke echoed her sister, bobbing her head up and down.

"I suppose so. Is this a trick to make us stay overnight?" Jennie's eyes met his again. "Along with ice skating on ponds, and horse and buggy rides, you also know a place where they can have S'mores?"

"Most definitely." He glanced at John and Louise silently seeking their permission. "Right here. We have the fire, and I have the sticks." He winked at the two girls. "Dipped in chocolate sauce."

"Awesome," Katie jumped off her chair. "Can we Papa? Can we stay and roast marshmallows?"

"Well, since I'm having coffee and pie, I don't see the harm in that. But we need to be out of here in an hour. Go see about you renting a car. While we're waiting, Jennie, why don't you give those insurance people a call and see what's happening with that adjustor. You can't be hanging around all day expecting him if he isn't going to show up." "I'll do that. I'll just step out for a minute."

Her mother nodded. "Makes sense. We'll take the kids home with us and you can get your rental car and swing by the police station and take care of that accident report. Without the distraction of two little girls around." Louise glanced at Nick. "I'll have a stick for S'mores too."

"You've got it, Louise," he said, sliding a hand on Jennie's back, guiding her toward the entranceway. Out of hearing distance from the girls, he said, "I guess we'll have to hold off on the skating until after the holidays. I didn't want to mention it in front of them, but I see your parents are anxious to leave soon."

"Yes, no skating today. But maybe on our return trip? Perhaps you could show me around and give me an idea on real estate prices in this area. It might be less expensive than living in the city."

"I'd like that. And trust me, it is cheaper. Safer too."

When Jennie made a move to go outside to make her call, he put a hand on her arm. "You can make the call right here, no sense stepping outside in the cold. There's only one other table left and they'll be leaving soon."

"Thanks." Her eyes twinkled at him. S'mores? Right here?" Her lips curved into a smile. "You're really something."

His pulse kicked into high gear. He thought she was really something too, and would like an opportunity to get to know her better. It had been a long time since he'd met someone that interested him this much. "I'll be closing the restaurant after you all leave. If you wouldn't mind my company I could tag along with you when you go to the police station. After all, I did give them the preliminary report. Then I could drop you off at one of the car rental places."

"Sounds good. I'd like that."

Nick left to get the cookies and sticks for the girls, and then returned in time to hear Jennie tell her parents that an insurance adjustor was out on another call but he hoped to make it to Heaven by four this afternoon.

"So, Mom, Dad, it looks like I'll be late. Don't hold dinner. I ate enough this afternoon. And I might help myself to a marshmallow or two."

Nick put the festive plate of shortbread cookies on the table, and handed out the sticks to the girls and Louise. "Better get one for you too."

"No need. My girls will share." She glanced at their excited faces, happy for the moment that they were enjoying themselves, and the accident was mostly forgotten.

"It might be close to your bedtime by the time I catch up with you all," she told her kids. "You promise to be good at Grandma's? You'll go to bed when you're asked, even if I'm not there to tuck you in?"

"Sure, Mommy." Katie took Brooke's hand. "Nana and Papa can read us our bedtime story. And we'll brush our teeth and everything." She grinned. "We will be so good that Santa will bring us lots of presents!"

"I'm sure he will," their grandmother said with a laugh. "And I can't wait for you to see our tree. We got an extra big one this year, and there's a small one in your room too."

"It's going to be the best Christmas ever," Brooke said, forgetting about her father for a minute. Then the smile left her sweet face. "But what about Daddy? He's in heaven. Why isn't he here?"

"It's not this Heaven," Katie answered, shooting her mother a look. "It's the one up in the stars."

"I think he's here," Brooke said with a stubborn tilt to her head. "Don't you?" she asked Nick, as if for support.

"Hard to say." He glanced at their faces, treading carefully. "I think people who've left us are always close by. They never go away completely...we just can't see them anymore."

"I want him here," Brooke said with a pout. "And I'm going to find him."

"He's right here," Nick pointed to her sweater, "in your heart. He'll always be with you. Anytime you want to talk to him, you can. Just because you can't see him, doesn't mean he can't hear."

"Mom says that too. Can I talk to him now?" she asked.

"That's up to your mom." He turned his eyes to Jennie and felt himself going into a downhill slide. Something about her called to him, and he didn't feel quite as complete as he'd always thought.

"Why don't you wait until you're home at Grandma's, honey? Bedtime, or when you're brushing your teeth, or having a bath. Quiet time works best." Jennie's auburn hair, just a shade darker than her daughters, caught the light from the fireplace.

Nick nodded. "I'll get the pie and the fixings for the S'mores, and then you all can be on your way." He was glad to be able to escape. The child looked near tears and he couldn't bear to see anyone cry. It had been hard enough listening to Jennie earlier, though she seemed happy now. His plan had worked.

He grabbed a package of marshmallows and a few more forks for roasting, and rushed them back out to the table. "Pie and dipping sauce coming right up. John, you think you can handle this S'more thing?"

"I've done it a time or two. Take your time with the pie. I might have my hands full for awhile."

Ally had given her last check to the table of girls who were getting ready to depart, then came to their table to remove their plates. She returned with small side dishes and warmed up chocolate sauce, then picked up a stick. "You girls must be very special," she said with an amused look. "We usually only do this late at night. Sometimes when everyone is gone, Nick, Byron and me put our feet up on the table and have a roasted marshmallow feast."

She glanced over at Byron who was getting ready to leave then turned back to them. "You guys need any help?"

With a grateful expression, John handed over the stick. "Looks like I won't have to wait for that pie after all."

An hour later the girls had eaten so many marshmallows and cookies they were getting sleepy. Nick had bustled back and forth between the fireplace and the kitchen, cleaning up and making sure that his dinner menu was well under way. He wouldn't have much prep time when he returned in a few hours.

John yawned and straightened up. "If we stay any longer we're all going to need a nap."

Louise stood. "I'll take the girls to the ladies room, and then we should be on our way." She glanced at her watch. "It's almost three."

"I'll take Jennie to the police station and to get her rental car. With any luck this adjustor will get here in good time and not keep her waiting." Actually he hoped that the adjustor didn't make it here at all. Maybe he could convince her to stay the night, if she didn't have the guilty influence of her parents and children around. But those thoughts were better kept unspoken.

What that would mean for the evening ahead he had no idea. He had no expectations, and very few wishes. But he hadn't been with a woman like her in a long while. He dated now and then, but it was mostly light-hearted fun between two consenting adults. He hadn't felt anything close to this good with any of them. Once before he'd felt a deep connection and thought he'd met the love of his lifetime, only to find out during their engagement that she was having an affair.

He knew Jennie wasn't ready to love again. She still grieved for her husband. Yet only a short while ago their eyes had connected as he'd popped a perfect golden marshmallow into her mouth. Her cheeks had grown warm and rosy and he knew with certainty that it wasn't the fire that had created her glow.

CHAPTER SEVEN

After the girls left with her parents, Nick locked the doors and Jennie followed him out back to his Jeep. He opened the passenger door and because it was a step up, he put a hand on her arm to help her in. She was five foot eight and probably could do well without his assistance, but she welcomed his touch and sweet attention. Was it Nick himself that made her hunger to be touched, or the fact that she missed her husband terribly—the human contact, or at least male human contact? She couldn't answer that question, and didn't care to explore it too deeply.

Instead, she smiled at him. "Thank you."

"My pleasure." When she was seated, he was still standing there watching her. Her heart skipped and she wasn't sure what she wanted. To bend over and kiss him? What would his lips taste like? Marshmallows and mint probably. She remembered his nearness as she sat bleeding in her car. His aftershave, his minty breath. She longed to taste his mouth to find out.

"What?" He grinned, his brown eyes flashing with humor. "You're staring at me like you have a question."

Her cheeks flushed. "I was? Sorry, I have all sorts of questions. I can't imagine why you're not married. No steady girlfriend?"

"No. I know a few girls in town, but no one special."

"Never been married? No little Nick juniors hiding in the wings?"

His grin widened. "No and no. Was engaged once. It didn't work out."

"Well, that was her loss." She pulled her coat around her a little more snugly, surprised by her boldness and almost ashamed of it too. "We better get going. You don't have long before you need to be back here."

"That's true." He closed her door and hopped around the back, sliding in beside her. He turned on the heat and glanced at the radio. "Christmas music or some country?"

"Who have you got?" she asked as he hit the CD player.

"Brad Paisley, LeAnne Rhimes, Faith Hill."

"Doesn't matter. I like them all." She gave him a quick smile. "I had to listen to Christmas tunes for four hours driving here. Must have heard "Here Comes Santa Claus and Frosty the Snowman at least a dozen times."

"Oh, that's just cruel."

"And unusual punishment," she added. "But it kept the girls happy and not squabbling. Then we had a big stretch of "I spy" that kept us amused for a good half hour. Guess we spotted about a dozen red cars, but no deer." She lowered her voice, "Brooke wasn't hoping to see a deer or a moose."

He laughed. "You're a good mother, and they are very sweet children." He darted his eyes toward her before they got on the highway. "Do you mind me asking what happened to their father?"

She licked her lips and her heart thudded fast. She hadn't talked about it for some time. Everyone in her circle of friends already knew. Talking about Daniel was never easy. She clasped her hands together and stared straight ahead.

She released a sigh, knowing it was an innocent question and one that deserved to be answered. "Daniel was a co-captain in the navy and he was on a training exercise. In Norfolk, where we live. His helicopter hit a flock of birds. It went down." She spoke in short, clipped sentences, keeping emotion out of it. Sticking to the details was essential in the telling of this story. "Everyone on board died. Six naval officers. That was last January." She glanced at his face to see how he was taking this news. "It was a routine training flight. They have hundreds a day. It was such a shock. I mean if he'd been in Afghanistan or something, one might expect a tragedy like this. But not here. Not on home turf." She blinked back tears and her voice was thick. "It was just so awful."

So much for keeping her emotions intact! But Nick deserved more than just her usual blurb. He was kind and caring, and willing or not, he was involved with her and the girls.

"Yes, it was." He darted her a glance.

"I'm sorry." She put a hand over her mouth. Nick swerved to the side of the road and gathered her close for a hug.

"I'm the one who's sorry," he said gently. "I shouldn't have asked."

She sniffed, but didn't pull away. "It's okay. I thought it would be easy telling you after all this time. And you have a right to know."

"You are a strong woman. Trust me, eventually the pain will lessen. You'll be happy again." He kissed the top of her head and ran a comforting hand down her back over the winter coat. "It has to be really tough on you and the kids. I'm glad you're moving back to Philly to be near your parents. It'll be good for all of you."

"Yes." She lifted her chin and her eyes met his. "You're so kind. Thank you." She fought the urge to sink her head in his chest and have a really good cry. The accident...the lack of sleep...she was mentally and physically exhausted. Her mother was right about that.

Instead she pulled away with a final sniff. He put the car in gear and got back on the road. "It shouldn't take long at the police station. We'll get you that rental car. Hope the adjustor doesn't keep you waiting."

"Me too. I'm wiped. Feel like I could sleep for hours."

"Maybe you'd be better off spending a night alone at the Inn. Get some rest. Christmas is a busy time, and you've been through quite an ordeal. Not just yesterday's accident, but for the whole year. You don't want to wear yourself out for the holiday. You'd be a happier Santa after eight hours of shut-eye."

After last night's terrible rest? "I know. If the guy's late, I just might do that."

"Here we are." He pulled into a parking lot where two squad cars sat in front of a small brick building. Heaven Police Station.

"This is it?" It was the size of a very small post office.

"It's more than they need." He cracked a smile. "We have no crime in Heaven. Not so much as a jaywalking ticket." Nick rubbed a hand over his jaw. "That's the truth, Jen. This is the safest place on earth."

"Nice," she said and opened her door. The crisp winter air caught her attention. "Okay. Let's get this done."

The initial report was pulled up in minutes and her information recorded. She was given a copy for her records and they kept the original. "That's all?" she asked.

"Yup. Told you. Easy as pie."

Then they were on their way to Hertz, and after a quick deliberation she decided on a Honda Pilot for the week. Plenty of room for the girls, booster seats and all.

He glanced at his watch and noticed it was close to four. "Well, that didn't take long. You'll be at the station in plenty of time, although the adjustor could start without you."

"I wonder what he does exactly? The mechanic already knows what's wrong. Does he just verify it?"

"Pretty much. He needs to do his own inspection for the insurance records, making sure they don't get ripped off. Want me to stick around? Everything's prepared for dinner tonight. No prep necessary."

"Wait a sec. It's my phone ringing." She dug into her purse and pulled out her cell. "Hello?" She listened as the adjustor told her he'd been held up and wouldn't be able to get there for at least another hour. "Five or five-thirty?" she asked, shooting Nick a glance.

"Hopefully," the man answered. "I'll do my best."

She ended the call without stomping her foot and put her phone away. "Small delay. I can probably hang at your restaurant for an hour," she told him, looking back at her rented vehicle.

"I have to run home and let the dogs out. Put some fresh food and water out for the night. Want to go for a ride? They won't mind the car in the lot. We can get it on the way back."

"Sounds good, but can we leave at the gas station? It would save me a trip." She could still be at her parent's by seven at the latest.

"Yeah. Of course."

She followed him to the station, parked her rental and climbed into his car. During the short drive she found herself curious to see where he lived. Where he worked was rustic and homey, his Jeep perfect for the mountains and snow.

He pulled up in front of a small cabin with a one-car garage. It was nothing special from the outside, but the neighborhood was nice. She heard a dog barking as he put the key in the door.

"That's Sammy. He's a little friendly. Are you afraid of dogs?"

"Not unless they bite," she answered with a smile. "Or run in front of my car."

"No. He's a lover not a fighter." Using his foot, Nick attempted to keep the big, white furry dog away from the door so they could enter. "Back Sammy."

"He's beautiful," Jennie said, squeezing past Nick who quickly got the door shut. Then a second dog came skidding around the corner and nearly knocked her over.

She recognized him from the accident. "You still have him. Are you going to keep him?" She bent over to pet the little guy. Sammy started sniffing her behind and then pushed his way between her and the pup.

"Get off me," she said, but gave him a hug and scratch too.

"I made some posters, and I was going to start putting them up around town but ran out of time. Last thing I need is another yappy mouth to feed." He picked up the pup, who barked happily, and snuggled into his shoulder to lick his neck.

"He loves you," she said, her heart sparking. "Look at that."

"I think he'd love your children more," he shot back.

"Not until we find a new place to live." She bit back a sigh at the things on her plate. Sometimes her problems seemed monumental, other times she handled them in stride. But of course, the holiday season added a whole new level of stress.

Her eyes roamed about the place which had built-in cabinets and a carved oval coffee table that didn't appear store-bought. It was stained polished wood and had a half moon base. It was pretty. Different. "Did you do that?" she asked, tilting her head to the table. "Are you a carpenter too?"

"I wouldn't call myself a carpenter but I like to work with my hands. I usually have a project or two going on. Keeps me occupied."

"I don't think you have any problem with that. Your restaurant doesn't give you much free time." Jennie pointed at the clock on the stove in the kitchen. "You've got to get back to work soon. I'm sorry that I took up so much of your time."

"I'm not." He opened up the sliding glass door and the dogs rushed out.

She walked into his living area, checking things out. For a bachelor he was very neat. The dogs had chewed up a magazine that might have been left on the floor, and a throw pillow on the sofa had a big hole in it with stuffing hanging out. She had a feeling that the puppy might be responsible for that.

"You have a nice place."

"It's okay. I'm just renting for now. My grandpa died last year and I've been trying to renovate the old farmhouse to put it up for sale. Then I might try to find something a little bigger for me." He stood at the back door, watching the dogs run around and play. "Good thing about this is the fenced yard, and convenience to everything."

"You don't want to keep the other house? The one you're renovating?"

"It's too big, and this is too small, so I'm looking for something just right." He put fresh food and water down for the dogs then let them back in. "I'm going to wash up," he told her. When he returned, he said casually, "If you're in the mood after the adjustor leaves, come by the bistro for dinner. Place isn't busy past eight."

"It'll be too late. I'll probably just drive home, but thanks for the offer."

"No problem. If something happens and you don't leave, give me a call or come by. Don't want you spending the night alone."

"I'll call, but I won't come by. Sleep sounds like a good idea. I'm exhausted. Barely slept at all last night, or the night before we left."

While the dogs were chowing down, the two of them slipped out the door. Ten minutes later they pulled into the garage at the gas station.

"Good luck with everything," he said, giving her a concerned look. "You do look tired. You sure that you want to drive into Philly tonight? You can leave first thing in the morning, and the kids will barely miss you."

She laughed. "I'm sure my parents are fussing over them right now, so you're probably right. I'll see how long this takes and make a decision then." She had her door open, but she leaned back to touch his arm. "Whatever happens? Don't expect to see me later."

"That's fine. I understand. But call me and let me know either way." His hair fell forward over his brow and he shoved it back. "Get some sleep."

"I could use it." She slipped out of the Jeep, the air now gray and cold. "Thanks for everything, Nick. Have a good night. I'll let you know when I'm on the road."

She knew he was still watching her as she strode toward the garage. Staying here tonight was tempting. He was tempting. But it was another complication and distraction that she certainly didn't need.

CHAPTER EIGHT

The gas station wasn't the nicest place to hang out and wait, but what other option did she have? Jennie went inside and grabbed a coffee. They had a small shop that sold snacks, drinks and convenience items. Not fancy, but it would do in a pinch. She explained to the guy behind the counter that she was waiting on an insurance adjustor and he told her she was welcome to wait as long as it took.

A half hour later, he gave her a worried look. "I think you're wasting your time, lady. Nobody's going to come out here this late. It's Saturday night before Christmas. The mechanic's gone home. I have a key to the garage, but only for emergencies."

Jennie tossed her cold coffee. "I know. I've called twice but didn't get through. It seems ridiculous to wait any longer. I'm sure he's not coming." Tears smarted her eyes and she wiped them away. She didn't normally cry at the drop of a hat, but she was emotionally exhausted. It was all too much, and she couldn't take it any longer. Nick was right. She needed a full night's rest, more than her kids needed her.

"I'm going to the Inn and see if I can get a room for the night. If by some stroke of good fortune this guy actually turns up, could you give me a call?" She wrote down her name and cell number on a piece of paper he gave her. "The adjustor's name is Allen Johnson."

"I'm Geoff," the pimply young kid told her. "I work until ten. If he calls or shows up, I'll be sure to let you know."

"Thanks, Geoff."

"You're welcome. I have the number for the Inn right here. I'll give them a jingle and let them know you're on your way."

"I appreciate that. Thanks so much." She had left her rental car in the gas station parking lot, and it was dark, the car unfamiliar, but she didn't have far to go. She already knew her way to Main Street, and it was at the end of the road.

As she passed Nick's Bar & Bistro, she felt a moment's longing, wishing she could stop for a reassuring hug that she knew would be fast in coming. But even more than his comfort, a few hours sleep was in order.

She parked outside the Inn, dragged her large suitcase out of the trunk and wheeled it into the lobby. When she stepped up to the check-in counter, a young woman smiled. "Ms. Braxton. Geoff let us know you were on your way. We've given you a room on the second floor. Room 204. Just need your signature and a credit card."

"Thanks so much. Everyone in this town is so welcoming." She forced a smile. "Never seen anything like it."

"My name is Helen Watson," the young girl replied. "I'm from Nebraska, and I've been here for two years. The friendliness is genuine, and it doesn't get old."

As Jennie's mother had said, the Inn was small, but charming—English Tudor in style both inside and out. The lobby had a tartan carpet, four plaid high back chairs next to a hearth and fireplace. The walls were decorated with hunting scenes and floral gardens. A small bar was tucked away in the far corner of the lobby, with a waiter dressed in a stiff white shirt, black vest and pants. One man sat on a stool, smoking a pipe and sipping on a port.

Jennie saw the elevator and stumbled toward it. As soon as she pressed the up button the door slid open and carried her to the second floor. Stepping off, she noticed the sign indicating room numbered 200-210 were on the right. The hallway was lit with wall lighting instead of glaring overheads, and the green and beige wallpaper was soothing to the eyes.

Hands trembling with fatigue, she got her door open and rolled her suitcase behind her. She didn't bother to unpack except for her toiletries and nightie.

Jennie made a quick call to her mother, informing her that the adjustor was so far a no-show, and that she had checked into the Inn, too tired to drive or to even think straight.

Louise agreed that that was the wisest and safest thing to do.

"Mom. Just need a quick nap, then I'll call you back and speak to the girls."

"Fine, honey. They're watching "How the Grinch Stole Christmas" with your dad."

Jennie laughed. Katie never got tired of that movie. "Good. Love you all, and will call back soon."

She ran a bath, adding some body wash to the water, hoping for bubbles. She stripped and stepped into the deep tub, closing her eyes with pleasure. Steam and hot water soothed her aches and worries, and she remained there until her bath was no longer warm.

Half asleep, Jennie put on her nightie, her cell phone on charge, and turned off the lights, sliding under the cool bed sheets for a nap. An hour's rest would do her more good than dealing with the insurance company or facing the 95 traffic right now. Everything she needed to do could darn well wait until morning.

Her eyes were closed, but the healing sleep didn't come. Little things ran through her brain. Nick's face floated to mind and wouldn't leave. His serious expression and his laughing one. Her stomach clenched remembering the look of concern in his eyes as he'd waited with her for the ambulance. How he'd smiled, popping out of his kitchen to check on them roasting marshmallows. Why wasn't he married?

He seemed to like children and was a kind man. What had happened? Why did he choose to live alone with only a dog for company?

He deserved happiness and she hoped one day he would open his heart and find it.

With that last thought, Jennie fell into a deep sleep.

When Jennie woke up the room was dark, and she could see from the clock next to her bed that it was almost eight. Two hours? She stretched and yawned, resting for a moment longer before getting up.

Christmas was always a busy, stressful time with presents to buy, finding the money to afford them, fighting for a parking spot in the mall, and getting the best deal and right gift for each and every loved one. She had presents for her parents, her sister and husband, and their two boys. She knew what little girls were into, but what did a ten and a twelve-year-old boy with a roomful of toys want that they did not already have?

When pressed, her sister had suggested something for their recently finished rec room. Like a hockey game or ping-pong table. Figuring that was an easy out, Jennie had bought the ping pong table online, set up a delivery time, and bought some racquets and balls as little gifts for under the tree. It certainly was less trouble than hunting down toys or sporting goods this time of the year.

Brooke and Katie were almost afraid of their rough and tumble bigger cousins, but she'd be there with them to referee and make sure that the boys were gentle. The last time her sister and nephews came to visit in Norfolk, the boys had broken the swing set and stuffed Lego pieces down the upstairs toilet. Boys will be boys, her sister had said, offering to pay to replace the swings and for the plumber. But that had hardly been the point.

How lucky she was to have two sweet daughters. She missed them already. She'd call them and wish them a good night, but she had promised Nick a call, and better do that first.

He'd given her his cell phone number so she didn't need to call the restaurant. He picked up right away. "Jennie! Where are you? I called the gas station and they said you'd left two hours ago. Are you home with your family?"

"No. I'm at the Inn. Guy never showed up. I waited until almost six and by that time I was so tired of hanging around I couldn't see straight. I just woke up."

"You're staying the night?"

"Yes. I couldn't face the drive."

"Want to come over here and keep me company?" His voice lowered. "I'll be closing up soon."

"Sorry, Nick. I'll take a rain check. I just want to sleep and sleep. And I still have to call the girls."

"Okay. I won't press you. I know how exhausted you are. I'll see you soon." He hung up.

She pondered that for a moment or two. Was he annoyed with her for not calling earlier? That was ridiculous! Why would he be? Well, she had too much to deal with right now than to worry about his sensitive feelings. And she wanted to hear her children's voices. Funny, how just after a few hours she missed them already.

"It's me, Mom. How's it going? Are the girls still up?"

"Yes. They're been waiting for your call. We had pizza for dinner, then they had their bath. They're in their PJ's, watching 'Charlie Brown's Christmas'."

Jennie smiled at the image. She knew how the girls loved watching movies and staying up past their bedtime. It was often a weekend treat—with popcorn, of course.

"Girls! It's your mom. Who wants to talk first?"

"Hi, Mom!" It was Brooke who'd reached the phone. "We watched the Grinch and now it's Charlie Brown. We're having popcorn. I love it here!"

Jennie laughed, sitting on the mattress and curling her feet beneath the covers. "Of course you do! Nana and Papa love having you, too." It was a big reason why she'd put her house on the market. "What else did you do today? Have you talked to your cousins?"

"Not yet. They're coming for Christmas though. Nana said we could go outside tomorrow and build snowmen. When are you coming? Maybe you could build a snowman too."

"I'd like that. Now, let me talk to your sister and then I have to make more pesky calls to the insurance people so I can come and be with you."

"Tonight?" she said hopefully.

"No, honey. Not tonight. But tomorrow. I promise."

"Okay. I love you, Mom."

"Love you more."

A second later Katie was on the line. "Hi, Mom. Where are you?"

"At the Inn. Where you stayed last night. I was so exhausted I fell asleep for two hours."

"You took a nap?" Katie asked. "Only Brooke takes naps."

"I was tired." She imagined Katie sitting with the phone to her ear, so grown up. "Now I'm going to make another call and see why the adjustor didn't show up. I want this all taken care of by morning." Get home to eat popcorn and watch movies with her kids.

"Okay, Mom. I love you. Nana wants to take us shopping. She says she wants to buy us something special. Whatever we want."

"And what do you want?" Jennie asked, knowing that she had everything covered on the girls' list.

"I don't know. I already asked Santa for everything."

"Okay. Well take it easy on Nana's pocketbook. Just pick out something small. Hopefully, I should be there and can come with you. Goodnight, sweetheart. I love you."

"Love you more. Here's Nana."

Her mom took the phone. "How did it go with you know who? The girls talked about him non-stop on the way home, so I don't want to say his name."

"Mom. Don't encourage them, please." She sat against the headboard. "You know how he is. Very supportive, but now he's at work. I'm in my PJ's and plan a big night watching TV."

"You've slept some. You should go to the bistro for an hour. I bet you haven't had anything since lunch. And you can walk there."

"I'm going to order room service. Listen, Mom, I should be home by noon. I have tons of presents for the girls, so you don't need to buy them anything else."

"I know, hon. But it will be fun to take them to the mall and look around. It's so beautiful right now with all the decorations. It might be a good idea to go early. Maybe we'll do that at nine, and be home by noon for lunch. They can do the snowman thing in the afternoon. That's a better plan."

"Okay. Have fun, and see you noonish."

"That's fine, dear. But I really wish you had better things to do. If you know what I mean."

"I do. And I don't." She sat on the edge of the bed. "I'm not ready for that yet, Mom."

"I know, honey. But don't wait too long. Sometimes we have to open the door when opportunity knocks."

"The only door I'm answering is room service. I still have to call the insurance adjustor. Again!" She sighed with growing frustration. "Got to go. Love you."

After she hung up, she ordered a turkey and Swiss sandwich and a glass of red wine to be brought to her room. Not as chic as the meals at Nick's, but it would do. She dressed in sweats and a t-shirt, and placed her last call for the evening to Allen Johnson who was still not answering her call. She left a message, saying she was at the Inn and would be available until morning.

She supposed she was lucky that anyone would be in touch with her before the holiday, but another delay was disappointing. Still, she had a car downstairs waiting for her, and she could spend the next few days with her family. If the adjustor had questions after seeing the car, it was a simple drive back.

Jennie sipped her glass of wine, feeling better about things already. She flipped around the TV channels and found an old movie that she'd previously enjoyed. She sat up on the bed with two pillows behind her, intending to watch the movie and then sleep.

A firm knock on her door made her sit up straighter and splash a little of her wine. Who in the world? Maybe it was housekeeping, wondering if she needed more towels. Or, the person who had dropped off her room service tray coming to collect. Or...or...no, it couldn't be!

She quickly glanced in the mirror just in case, and winced when she saw her reflection. Navy sweats and an old Gap tee, no bra, no make-up. Hair a mess from the way she'd slept. So not good. It better be housekeeping.

She opened the door a crack and peeked through the opening.

"Jennie! I tried to call you back, but you didn't answer your phone. So here I am in the flesh. I brought you a big container of clam chowder in case you're hungry."

"Nope. But thanks. I had room service."

"How are you feeling?" He squinted at her. "You look rested."

"A little better, but it's going to take more than a couple of hours sleep. Sorry I didn't answer your call, but I was talking to the kids, then left a message for Allen from the insurance company." She curled her toes into the carpet, not budging from behind the door.

He shook the melting snow from his brown hair. "Ally and Byron are closing for me," he said with a mouthwatering grin, "and I have a surprise for you. When you didn't answer I was afraid that maybe you'd already left. The surprise is downstairs." His eyes glittered with excitement, like one of her kids. "Won't you please open up?"

"I'm a mess. Go away." She tried to hide behind the door. His grin was too charming, and he looked delicious. Maybe the sandwich hadn't satisfied her appetite because she really wanted to lick that cleft in his chin.

"What?"

"That's rude of me, and I'm sorry," she said, hand holding the door firm. "You've already been kind enough. I'm just too exhausted for another surprise."

Unexpectedly, he gently pushed at the door, and she stepped back with a squeak. Still grinning, he walked in. "I can't take no for an answer."

His assertive side was kind of sexy, she thought, surprised at her reaction. "Oh?"

"So, get dressed." He folded his arms and looked at her. Head to foot. A slow, heated perusal that left her feeling on fire. "You look fine, but you'll need something warm. Jeans and a sweater will do."

"What are you planning?" she asked cautiously. "I wanted to go to bed early. I'm still exhausted."

A wicked gleam came into those beautiful brown eyes. "That could be arranged. If you insist."

"Nick!" Hands folded at her waist, Jennie stared at this dangerously sexy man in front of her. Where had the nice guy gone? Had it all been an act?

He laughed, brushing her cheek with a light touch of his knuckles. "Don't look so surprised. You're the one who suggested it. Not me."

"I didn't mean us," she said with a hot blush. "Not you and me. Just me."

"Okay. Perhaps I misunderstood." He advanced toward her. One step at a time. When he was a foot away, he looked down at her. She was about six inches shorter than him without shoes. "One hour," he said in a soft, caressing voice. "That's all I'm asking. I'll have you back here at ten. How's that?"

Jennie didn't know what he'd planned, but it would be rude of her to say no. After all, he'd made arrangements, wanting to please her, she justified to her rapidly beating heart. "I suppose." She cleared her throat, feeling a little breathless. Slowly, she lifted her gaze to his and ran a hand through her messy hair. "Do I need make-up?"

"Nope. You're beautiful just as you are." His eyes dropped and she wondered if he could see through her thin Gap shirt. Her nipples tightened in response.

"Where exactly are you taking me?"

"Come see for yourself." He winked, and gave her rear end a light tap. "Off you go. Change into something warm."

"Are you always this pushy?" she asked, heading toward her suitcase.

"Yes." He paused, his brown eyes darkening. "When I want something."

She took her clothes into the bathroom, wondering exactly what it was that Nick might want. She shivered as she tossed her tee onto the tub, and then caught a glimpse of her naked breasts. Even though they were small and perky, they felt heavy, swollen with need. She touched them lightly and felt a physical reaction. Her body was sensual again.

It had been dead for the past year, but now it was singing a new melody, and Jennie wasn't sure if she liked it or not.

She left her bra on the tub and slipped the heavy wool sweater over her head. The rough texture rubbed her breasts, making her feel sexy. She put on a skimpy pair of lace undies and her jeans, brushed her teeth and her hair, then smiled at her reflection. Her eyes were shiny and bright. Cheeks pink, and flushed with pleasure.

Always a mom, tonight she remembered she was a woman, too. Alive. And just maybe she'd enjoy a first kiss.

CHAPTER NINE

Nick waited in the hotel room, wondering what Jennie was thinking behind the closed bathroom door.

She'd blushed, adorable and caught off-guard, in her sweats and bare feet.

He hadn't wanted Jennie to leave in the morning, not without seeing him tonight. She was alone. No kids around. The opportunity was too good to miss. It had occurred to him several times as he'd prepared people's meals, that she might leave and he'd never see her again. It shouldn't matter, but for some reason it did.

That scared him, but not enough to back away. He wanted to pursue whatever it was that was driving him toward her, to explore the emotions that she had mysteriously lit. Not that he was an unemotional guy. He just hadn't felt this much compassion, or warmth—whatever the hell it was—for a lady in awhile.

Jennie was different. He didn't need to have sex with her to want to make her happy. The fact that she had two adorable children and no husband made him feel protective. Yeah, that was it. He didn't want some asshole sweeping in and taking her to bed, only to leave her with a broken heart.

Right or wrong, he wanted to be her champion, and he totally understood that she'd fight him every step of the way if she knew his feelings. Not that he would turn down an opportunity to make love to her, he wasn't that much of an idiot, but it wasn't the driving force that led him to call the hotel and make sure she hadn't checked out.

"Do I need a hat?" she called through the door.

"Yeah." He sat on the edge of the bed. When he discovered she was still there, he'd called Darcy, the buggy driver, to ask a favor. He was a regular at Nick's Bistro, so Nick promised him a free dinner for himself and his family, and a very generous tip.

Darcy was happy to oblige. He had chuckled, and told Nick that he must have met his lady-love. Nick had laughed back, but he hadn't been amused. Hadn't changed his mind, though, either.

When she popped out of the restroom, he glanced at her with approval. She'd brushed her pretty hair out, added some gloss to her mouth, and something glittery to her eyes. "You look perfect for an evening stroll."

"We're going for a walk?" She swept by him to the closet where she'd hung her coat and scarf.

"Do you always spoil surprises?" He got up, liking the color in her cheeks.

"No...but..."

He put an arm casually around her waist and led her toward the door. "Grab your gloves, too. You'll need them."

She gave him a skeptical look. "I wish you'd just tell me."

"I'll tell you this much. You look beautiful." He sniffed behind her ear and stopped himself from nibbling. Barely. "Is that perfume? Smells like berry."

"No. It's the liquid bath soap I used in the tub."

"Aw. You just painted a picture in my mind."

She glanced at him. "Then get it out. I mean it! I don't want you seeing me naked."

"It's only in my thoughts," he said with a shrug.

"Still. I've had two children. I'm not the young, sexy thing you're probably visualizing anyway."

He let his eyes graze over her. "I don't think you'd disappoint me, not that I plan to find out."

"Good. Glad to hear it."

He laughed. "Here's your hat. Put it on."

"Bossy." She grabbed the hat, and stuffed it on her head so that it covered half her face. "There. How's that?"

"Warm. And cute." He helped her on with her jacket, enjoying being so close to her. She looked adorable, all the more so because she was angry, and confused, and maybe a little exited too. Her eyes were sparkling and she didn't pull away when he touched her.

When she was ready, he ushered her out the door, making sure he had the key so she wouldn't be locked out. In silence, they took the short flight down to the first floor. She pranced through the lobby and out the door then stopped short when she reached the street.

"Really?" She turned to him. "You did this? The carriage ride...really?"

He wasn't sure if she was upset or pleased. "Yes," he said cautiously, trying to see her head-on. "I promised to put a smile on your face today but you didn't have much to smile over." He lifted her chin, staring into her green orbs for the truth. "Is this okay? If you don't want to go, I'll cancel it."

"No." She sniffed and her eyes glistened with tears. "It's just terribly sweet and no one has wanted to do something this nice for me in a long while. I don't know why you do."

"Because I like you. I know you're having a difficult time, and if I can do one thing to make it better, then I'm happy to oblige." He took her hand, squeezing her gloved fingers. "Darcy, this is Jennie. She's new in town. Why don't we take her down Main Street and let her see how pretty it is with all the fairy lights? I promised her we'd be back by ten."

"Hi Darcy. Thanks for doing this." She patted the horse's reddish brown mane. "What's his name?"

"Rusty. Not too original considering he's a chestnut."

She smiled. "Hey, Rusty. Sorry to keep you out so late. I'm sure you're both tired."

"Not at all," Darcy answered. "It's my pleasure, Jennie. I hope you like it here in Heaven. Most people do."

Nick helped Jennie into the open carriage, and then sat next to her. He put a plaid blanket over both their legs, and held her gloved hand between his.

"I know you saw the main drag during the day, but it's really special late at night. There's something almost magical about this town, especially at Christmas." He turned to look at her profile. "Most people feel that way about where they live. New Yorkers believe it's the greatest city in the world, and Philadelphia has lots to boast about too. But this place is better. You'll see."

Jennie's long auburn hair trailed down the back of her winter jacket as she turned her head. "It is simply beautiful. All the twinkly lights on the trees and store windows. The candy striped lanterns. You're right about it being magical at night. It's like a postcard."

"Told you so." The horse clomped along the cobblestones, carrying them past Nick's restaurant. "I was lucky to get this location. Would have been tough running a restaurant that wasn't on Main Street."

"Was it a restaurant when you took it over?" Jennie curled her fingers around his and made his heart beat double-time.

"It was. More of a coffee shop that catered to the morning and early afternoon crowd. They had booths and the long bar was a counter service. They served sandwiches, soups, and breakfast."

"Oh." She tilted her head, her pretty mouth in a pink bow as she peeked at him. "Well, I like it better now."

Her flirting glance about killed him. He kept his tone light. "You're just saying that because you like me."

She smiled and bumped shoulders with him. "I do like you."

"That's a good start," he answered, wondering why he had to fight the urge to kiss her. Normally, he'd do just that. Romance literally glittered in the night air. But because she was a widow, he respected her, and didn't want to do anything that might be misconstrued.

"What is it about you?" She turned on her seat to face him, adjusting the blanket across their laps. "You're not like most men."

"In what way?" Funny thing was, he'd heard that most of his life. He was different. Always had been.

"I don't know. It's like you want to be friends, without any of the usual sexual strings. Is that even possible?"

He blinked. Talk about saying it straight. "Well, you know. You're a young widow and I'm sure many guys will be all over that. But I don't think you're ready to be romanced." Nick leaned back against the cool wooden bench. "If you were, you'd have already come on to me."

"Is that right?" She flipped her hair over her shoulder, her mouth torn between a smile and a scold. "Got quite a high opinion of yourself, don't you?"

"Just telling the truth." She'd started the honest conversation and he wanted to keep it going. "I've had my share of women that would like to know me better. They were hardly subtle."

"And how well did they succeed?" She eyed him with curiosity, as if trying to make her mind up about him. If only he knew what she wanted to know, deep down inside her heart, then he could show her better what was inside his.

"Well, I'm still single. Some folks around here think I'm gay."

Her brows flew upward behind the brim of her hat.

"Other's think I'm a confirmed bachelor. Truth is— I'm neither. I just haven't met the woman I want to spend the rest of my life with." Her hands stayed folded above the blanket at her lap. As much as he wanted to hold them, he left them there. "I have a new business to run. No time or inclination to look."

"So why are you here with me?" She twisted around in the seat to give him a direct look. "Still feeling guilty because I smacked my car into a tree?"

"No...I..."

"You what?" She held his gaze, her mouth in an inviting pout. "Do you want to kiss me, or don't you?"

His mouth fell open and he slammed it shut. He was struck dumb. Was that an invitation? It sure sounded like one. And her eyes were twinkling. Of course he wanted to kiss her. He was a hundred percent male. And she was a very attractive woman, who was now smiling at him, waiting for a response.

He slid his arm around her shoulder and pulled her closer. "What do you think?"

And then, he kissed her.

CHAPTER TEN

His kiss was light at first. Explorative. Not dominating or intrusive, but like a man who wasn't sure if his kiss would be welcome. Jennie kissed him back, letting him know that it was. She hadn't been kissed by anyone but her husband in ten years, and she had forgotten how one man's lips could be sweeter than another. Nick's lips were firm at first, but then softened and his breath was like honey. She felt heat between them, enough she hoped to melt the icicles around her heart.

He slanted his head and deepened their kiss. She held on to his shoulders, accepting and giving in response. As much as she welcomed the taste of his lips and the slow burn stirring inside of her, she didn't want to be ravished, or be like the other women he knew who wanted him and let their wants be known.

Hell no. She might be a widow, but she wasn't desperate. Not with two sweet daughters to share her life with. But the girls weren't here right now, and Nick was, so she might as well enjoy the next hours. He had promised to put a smile on her face, and by damn, he was!

She pushed away and gave him an inquisitive look, unsure if she wanted to proceed or retreat. "That was nice. Thank you."

His lips twitched. "You're welcome. Would you like another one?"

"In a minute." She sucked in a breath, feeling the chill of the cold night air. There were plenty of stars in the sky, adding another magical illusion to this fairytale night. Here she was, snuggled in a blanket, on a carriage ride heading for an unknown park beside a handsome, charming man who only wanted her to be happy.

Was that the best thing or what! How did she get so lucky to crash into that tree and end up here? Whoa. Wait a minute. If that hadn't happened she'd be with her parents and children right now, sitting next to a fireplace and watching the Grinch.

She looked at him, trying to decide which was better.

"What?"

"Just thinking. I could be with my kids watching Christmas cartoons right about now. Instead, I'm here with you."

"Any regrets?"

"About the kiss? No. Or the carriage ride." Her eyes met his. "This was a wonderful surprise. Thank you."

He put an arm around her shoulder, and pulled her in close. She snuggled into him, and even dropped her head against his shoulder. It was strange to trust this man. But she did. Completely.

He gently kissed the top of her head. She pulled the woolen cap off and stuffed it between her knees. Then she turned her face again, lifting it to look into his eyes.

Her heart skidded and faltered. What was she doing? Was she ready to take a chance?

Before she could answer that question she rushed ahead, wanting to embrace the moment, for good or bad. "I'm ready for a second one now."

His eyes burrowed into hers, as if wanting to read her mind, but her mind was flopping all over the place, so he wouldn't learn much. She pulled his head toward her and kissed him. At first tentatively, but then she grew restless, and wanted more than that. She wanted to taste his sweetness.

His tongue met hers, and the fire inside of her sparked into a flame. Her fingers splayed into his hair, holding his head so that she could lay claim to his mouth. He might not like the women who wanted him, and after this evening he might not want her again. But tonight he was hers. For this hour. Until ten o'clock, and then like a pumpkin the carriage would deliver them home, and he'd be gone.

Leaving not so much as a shoe.

She giggled.

"Now what?" he murmured, his mouth nibbling down to her neck.

"I feel like Cinderella. At the stroke of ten, this magic will be over."

"It doesn't have to end."

Her insides exploded. With want. With need.

"Yes, it does. But we still have some time left." She rolled her head back, loving the feel of his tongue, his teeth, as he kissed and nipped the length of her neck and then took her mouth once more.

94

She opened her mouth, taking his tongue, and plunging with her own. The kiss was electrifying, sizzling her from the tips of her toes to the hairline. Soul-deep kisses that would warm her memories for many nights to come.

Finally, she gasped, unable to breathe. Her eyes widened as she gazed beyond him at the sky. "Look at the moon. It's almost full. So big and bright. Did you arrange for that too?"

"Of course I did. I wanted a perfect night for you."

"I see why you're popular," she said with a teasing grin. "Do you make all your ladies feel this special?"

"No. And I don't have any ladies to speak of. Present company excluded." His hands played with the strands of her hair. "Last summer there was someone. But it only lasted a few months. She went back to California."

"Her loss," Jennie answered, and kissed him once more.

The ride through the park was lovely, although too dark to see much except the same pretty lamp posts that were on Main Street, and a lake that was frozen over. She imagined that was the popular skating pond, but at this hour it was deserted.

He squeezed her hand. "Close your eyes. I have one more surprise."

She did as he asked, wondering what more he could offer her.

"Okay. Open them now."

When she did, she gasped. There was a huge Ferris Wheel all lit up, and a lovely carousel too. Oh, how the children would love this!

"Unbelievable! This is so sweet, and amazing. No wonder you wanted me to see your park. And why you love Heaven so much."

"What's not to love? We have everything we need a half hour away, but here we have something the city can't offer. A communal sense of how life should be—a peaceful existence, with security, and serenity."

Her insides rumbled. It would be easy to live here, but she'd hate to relocate the children and then find out that this was all a fantasy. Or that Nick's interest in her wasn't real. Not that he'd be the number one reason she'd move here, of course. But how would it be to see him every day and not have his arms to depend on?

She sat back, putting a little distance between her and Nick on the return ride. He seemed content to hold her hand and not ask for anything more. He was a wise man, she decided. Too wise to ask for things he shouldn't, and to take only what was offered.

When the carriage stopped in front of the Inn, Nick jumped down and held out his hand. She accepted his help, then thanked the driver, and again patted the horse.

"It was an amazing ride," she told Darcy. "Thank you so much. I loved every minute."

"Anytime." He doffed his cap. "Hope to see you again soon. Have a lovely night now."

"I will." She turned to thank Nick but he was standing at the doorway of the hotel, holding the door for her to enter.

"You don't need to come in," she said, brushing past him, feeling her heart flutter like a trapped bird.

"I would love a nightcap. Won't you join me?"

96

She saw the bar was still open, and two other people were seated at a small cozy corner table sipping on a hot whipped cream drink.

"That looks delicious," she said. "Okay." Jennie didn't want the magic to end. What harm would another half hour do? She could sleep in the morning. No kids to worry about. When was the last time she had that? The day before they were born?

They ordered Kahlua coffees and sat in the cozy armchair by the window. His long legs were stretched out under the table and his feet touched hers.

She set her drink on the low table. "I can't thank you enough."

"Did I make you happy?" he asked, his eyes dropping to her mouth and flushed cheeks.

Oh yeah! It had been a long time since she'd been kissed like that. Even though she and Daniel had been happily married, their kisses had grown less passionate. Tonight had made her feel young again, starry-eyed, explosive, like rockets and flares were going off. She smiled, her heartbeat picking up again. "Very."

"That's all the thanks I need."

"I'm going to miss this town when I'm gone," she said simply, knowing she'd miss him too. But she needed to get back to her kids and family and reality, and the numerous responsibilities that being a single parent brings.

"You're leaving in the morning?" Nick put his hands around the hot glass mug, his eyes on the whipped cream and not her face.

"I am. It's Sunday and the insurance adjustor never called me back. It's doubtful that I will hear anything until Monday. Not sure if we will meet then, or after Christmas. So there is no reason for me to hang around here. It's only a half hour drive."

"That's true." He picked up his spiked coffee and took a big sip, then wiped the whipping cream off his lips. "Drop by if you do get back here in the next few days, or when you return for your car. I'd like to see you and the kids again."

"I'd like to see you too." She looked at him, wondering if he could be the one. She didn't feel ready to love again, but her children needed a father in their lives, and one day she would have to open her heart and share her bed. She almost wished it could be him.

"Good. Don't forget, I have a house for sale. After the holidays, and before you buy something else, you might want to take a look."

"I might." She smiled, feeling better knowing that she had a solid reason to see him again. "Before I make an offer on anything I need to have my Virginia house sold. I priced it well, and hopefully it should sell before summer. That would be the ideal time to move."

"Agreed. So you won't be moving quite yet? For some reason, I thought you were in a hurry to relocate."

"No. I want the kids to finish the school year where they are. This holiday I want to spend some time looking around at areas and homes to see what is available, and what I can afford. Plus I'd need at least two or three month's closing time for my home, and also the one I'd be buying."

"That makes sense." He finished his coffee, his eyes on her face,

She drank hers slowly, half wishing the night didn't have to end.

"It's been a long time since I enjoyed myself so much." She pushed the cup aside and batted back tears. "What are you doing for the holidays? Is your restaurant open for Christmas?"

He smiled. "No. We're sold out Christmas Eve, and then we stay closed until the 28th. I wanted to give Ally and Byron a few days off in case they want to go visit family." He shrugged. "Ally's been with me a year, Byron two, and yet they never talk about their family. I asked a few times, but they just shrug it off."

"Well, that being the case, maybe you should join us for Christmas dinner. I know my parents would love to have you. And the kids would enjoy it too." The words were spoken impulsively but she knew it was true. The only thing she hadn't added was how much his visit would mean to her.

"How about you?" he asked slowly.

She held his look. "Please come. I might find us some mistletoe."

"Confirm with your family," he said with a smile. "And then give me a call." He pulled out his wallet and handed her a business card with the restaurant number and his own personal cell. "Anytime."

Her heart jumped and skidded. She swallowed nervously. Oh my, but he did things to her insides. It was deliciously scary.

"I will." She pushed herself out of the comfortable chair, knowing she'd better leave before asking him to stay. "Thanks for everything."

"Drive safely tomorrow. Take care."

They looked at each other, and she very much wanted to kiss him. But not here in the lobby under bright lights. It had been a magical thing on the carriage ride, and she didn't want to sully the image now. If they kissed again, she wanted it to mean something. To be real.

"Goodnight, Nick." She turned and fled.

CHAPTER ELEVEN

Jennie woke up the following morning feeling refreshed after a long night's sleep. She couldn't remember the last time she'd slept so well, but she knew it was before Daniel's accident. Just like everyone in the world remembers where and what they were doing when the terrorists attacked the Twin Towers, that phone call telling her that her husband's copter went down was firmly etched in her memory.

She'd been picking up groceries from a local upscale market, selecting her organic vegetables and salads when her cell phone rang. She had her cart half full. Organic chicken, and meats, a loaf of fresh bread, cereal, treats for the kids and her sweet-toothed husband.

Then she answered the damn phone. In a solemn voice someone informed her that they were very sorry, but Captain Daniel Braxton and Captain Jerry Sloane and two staff sergeants were tragically killed in a training exercise. It was confirmed that there were no survivors.

Her world had gone black. She woke up on the floor of the produce section, a stranger peering into her face. And nothing had ever been the same again.

She stretched and flipped over, not eager to leave the cozy warmth of the bed and luxurious duvet. The clock next to her said it was seven thirty, but she didn't need to rush anywhere. Her family expected her around noon.

She hugged her pillow, eager to expand this rare moment when she had no obligations and places to be, but could simply explore her thoughts and analyze her feelings. Yes, her world had changed, and this past year had been a very difficult one. This move was a good decision as she needed a fresh start and a chance to rebuild her life over. It would be sad to leave their friends behind and the house that had brought her so much joy when Daniel was alive, but now the house was filled with memories. It was time to make new ones and stop living in the past.

Her mind flickered back to Nick and the special night he'd given her. The kiss. She wiggled her toes as she remembered the feel of his lips and the honeyed taste of his mouth. He was yummy. And she might see him at Christmas.

The thought brought a smile to her face. She knew her mother would be delighted, and her dad more cautiously so. Her sister would be all over him, wanting to know everything at once. She cared deeply about Jennie's happiness and worried about her and the children.

While Christy grilled Nick, her husband, Matt, would sit back and quietly make his own assessment. He was easy going, warm, caring and bright. Her father and Matt enjoyed each other's company, and both took a back seat when it came to their wives.

Jennie pushed the duvet back and slipped out of bed. She needed to use the bathroom and grab a cup of coffee before she planned her morning. After using the facilities, she found the two cup coffee maker and set it to brew.

While she waited she opened the curtains just enough to see what Heaven's weather would bring them today. Not surprising, the sun was out, glistening on the pure white snow. How could one place be so perfect, she mused, when the rest of the country was suffering from major catastrophes? Only days ago there had been terrible mudslides in California, a hurricane along the Jersey Shore, and a tornado in Kansas.

Nick had described life here as a peaceful existence, with security and serenity. Lord knew, she and the girls could use some of that. But she needed to get a decent job, and Philadelphia offered so much more opportunity-wise. It made sense to be close to her parents, as they were getting older and if anything happened to one of them, she could be there lickety-split. Also, having her parents within a ten or fifteen minute drive would mean free babysitting on demand, and to see them at will.

The scent of freshly brewed coffee beckoned her, and she poured herself a cup. She sat up in bed, pillows behind her, sipping on the coffee, and turned the TV on to NBC, reporting from Philadelphia's news station. The coffee splashed in her hand when she heard the lead story this morning. There had been another random shooting in a mall full of city shoppers—the alleged shooter had been apprehended, leaving the aftermath of several people dead, and twelve injured.

Her children needed to be kept safe. And if this wholesome little town could give them a sense of security then perhaps this was the answer after all. *Right, Daniel?* "You did this, didn't you?" The feeling gave her a warm buzz. "Either this is a small detour from my life's journey, or it's the reason we ended up here."

When she didn't hear an answer, she finished her coffee and went in to shower. Later, once she was fully dressed, she called down for room service, ordering a cheese omelet and whole wheat toast. Then she sat down to call her mother.

"Good morning, Mom. How are the kids?"

"They're enjoying the pancakes Papa made for them. He even made a smiley face with blueberries, then topped it off with whipping cream and syrup on the side."

"Oh my. They are getting spoiled." She added, "Keep up this treatment, my girls won't want to come home with me."

"It is such a pleasure having them. They are so well behaved and sweet as can be."

"Thank you. I think so too." She hesitated for a moment, then sucked in a breath, and released it in a rush. "Well, you'll never guess what I did last night. I was so tired that I slept half the night, and ordered a sandwich in."

"That sounds a little lame," her mother said. "Didn't you see Nick?"

"Well, that's where the surprise came in. He showed up at the Inn around nine. With a horse and carriage." She laughed, feeling the excitement all over again. "Can you imagine? I didn't show up at the restaurant so he brought the buggy ride to me."

"How romantic," her mother murmured. "He is a very sweet man."

"Yes. Well, the driver's name was Darcy. Isn't that perfect! And he took us down Main Street." She sighed and put a hand to her chest. "It was so pretty at night with all the lights and street decorations, and the park was amazing. I need to tell the girls something. Can you put them on?"

A second later, Katie answered. "Hi, Mommy. We're eating breakfast. Papa makes better pancakes than you do. It's got whipping cream!"

"I'm glad. Enjoy it now because when we get home it'll be back to school and only time for porridge, or an egg sandwich."

"I know. Do you have a car? Are you coming here now? We could save you a pancake."

"I'll be there in a couple of hours. I have to do a little more shopping for a couple of special people."

Katie giggled. "Me and Brooke?"

"Yes, and Nana and Papa."

"Okay. We're going to a mall too. Maybe it'll be the same one."

"I hope not. Don't want to ruin your surprises. But I'm calling because I wanted to tell you something. It's really special."

"What?" Her young voice rose with excitement.

"There's a very cool park here in Heaven and it has a carousel and a Ferris wheel!"

"Wow! Can we go on it? Can we?"

"Well, I'm pretty sure you can. If it's running during the winter. I couldn't tell because it was late at night. Nick took me on a carriage ride."

"Are you going to marry him?"

Jennie choked on her coffee. "No, honey, of course not! Why do you ask?"

"Because he's nice and I wouldn't mind if you did."

"Oh, sweetheart." This was why single mom's didn't date. "I barely know him."

"I know, but he seems to like us. And he's a good cook!" she added, as if that might seal the deal.

"Everyone likes you and your sister, because you are both so sweet, and clever and nice."

"You're just saying that 'cause you're our mom."

"I'm saying it because it's true and I love you both more than anything."

"Love you too, Mom. Want to talk to Brooke? Her mouth is full of pancake."

"Okay. Tell her to swallow."

"Hi, Mom. Did you say something about a Ferris wheel? Where?"

"Here in Heaven. In the park. When we come back to pick up the car, maybe we could all go for a ride on it. If it's up and running."

"Nick too?"

"No, Nick will probably be busy working."

"Well, we like him. And Grandma does too. I heard her telling Auntie Christie all about him."

"I'm sure she did, but Brooke, even though we all like him, we don't know him very well." Jennie had made the call to ask her mother about inviting Nick for Christmas.

Now she had to reconsider. She didn't want her children or her family getting the wrong idea. He didn't seem like the marrying kind, and she wasn't ready even if he was. Perhaps it would be best for everyone not to invite him after all. She could make up a simple excuse. He wouldn't mind. Might even be relieved. Although the memory of his kiss and the way he'd looked at her when he said goodnight, told her differently.

She heard a knock on the door and welcomed it. She had a lot to consider.

"My breakfast just got here," she told her daughter. "Tell your grandma that I'll be home by noon. I need to make a couple of stops." This was a great opportunity to finish up her shopping without the kids in tow. "See you later, kiddo."

She opened the door, took the tray from the young man's hands and gave him a tip. Carrying the tray inside, she placed it on the bed until she could make room on the small table next to the window. She refilled her coffee pot, and took the lid of her omelet, thinking about the conversation, knowing what she needed to do. Her exuberance faded and she felt a knot tighten in her stomach. Her parents and sister and family would love to have the children near, and she needed their emotional support.

Heaven was a wonderful town, but it wasn't practical for her to think about buying a house here. And Nick was only the first man she'd been attracted to since Daniel's death. It was natural that his kiss and flirtation had gone to her head. Well, she needed to get out of town and clear it so she could get back on the right path.

Number one, she had to get a good job again. Daniel's pension wouldn't be enough, and even if it were, she needed to be occupied while the children were in school. But the only job she'd ever had was working for the airlines, and she couldn't do that again. Not flying anyway. She might enjoy a job as ground personnel, and work at an airport—except for the fact it would be killer hours, and she'd need a nanny. That would never work. She had no idea what she wanted to do with her life. But she needed to figure it out soon. And she would, once she resettled.

She ate a few bites from her breakfast, but she'd lost her appetite. The thought of calling Nick, and not seeing him again, weighed heavily on her heart. She wanted him. For herself. He made her feel good. After a year of mourning, it was nice to feel alive and happy again. He had given her that. She knew it was a temporary gift, but now she didn't even have that to look forward to for Christmas.

Inviting him would be a mistake. For the kids, for her family, and perhaps more importantly, for herself. She was vulnerable right now. Especially this holiday season. Once she got through this, and returned to Norfolk to finish off the school year, she'd forget about this lovely place, and the taste of Nick's kisses, the warmth of his smile, and the shining light in his eyes as he made S'mores for her and the kids.

For her own serenity, she had to.

CHAPTER TWELVE

Nick felt a rough tongue on his cheek and opened his eyes slowly. He'd been dreaming of Jennie and their kisses, and went to wrap his arms around his frisky female, but encountered a hairy mutt instead.

"What the heck?" He pushed the dog off him. "What am I going to do with you? I need to hang those posters up around town. Find you a good home. And no. It's not mine." He looked into the dog's eager eyes and saw his tail wag joyfully. "You're a good little rascal and I'm sure someone will want you. Don't you worry. Meanwhile, let me take you outside so you don't mess up my place."

He slipped out of bed and into his robe and slippers and found a big wet spot in front of the patio doors. "Oops. Guess I'm too late." He opened the door for Sammy and Rasco, thinking that was as good a name as any. Then he got a roll of heavy duty paper towels and stooped down to mop the floor. Once it was dry, and after his coffee, he'd use a wood cleaner and a mop. Later.

He made his coffee and turned on the TV news, horrified to see the report about the shooting in the mall.

He didn't miss the city a bit. It was there for the nights when he wanted something out of the ordinary, or needed something he couldn't buy here, but for the most part, he was perfectly happy living the quiet life.

Once he got his grandparent's old farmhouse up to snuff, he'd unload that and get himself a nice bungalow on the outskirts of Heaven. A custom built log cabin would be kind of cool, but he didn't mind the idea of a planned new development. One day he'd probably marry and have kids of his own, and he didn't want to have to sell again and go to the hassle of moving. Best if he planned for that now.

He sipped on his coffee, thinking about Jennie and her kids. They were a beautiful family, and one day she'd meet Mr. Right and remarry. He'd bet it wouldn't take long. She was a hellava kisser, and had felt damn good in his arms. So much so, that he couldn't wait to see her again. Christmas was not a good day to spend alone. He and his grandpa had stopped celebrating once Grandma had died, and they'd go grab a ready-made turkey dinner from the local grocery. They would exchange a store bought sweater and laugh affectionately about the ugly Christmas sweaters Grandma used to knit for them. They never wore them again.

It would be fun to be around a real family for Christmas day. A real tree, lots of presents and laughter and kids. He could aleady smell the familiar scents coming from the oven. Turkey basted in butter and herbs, savory homemade stuffing, side dishes of sweetened yams and mashed potatoes, green bean casserole, cranberry sauce. They might serve pumpkin pie after, or a delicious pecan pie. It had been years since he'd had a home cooked dinner like that. He didn't cook them either. They closed on Christmas Eve and remained closed until the 28th. He never asked about Byron's plans or Ally's, not wanting to pry. If they wanted to tell him, they would.

Rasco barked, so he opened the door and let the two dogs in. He filled their bowls with a mixture of canned beef and dried kibbles and watched them dig in. Rasco was eating out of an old margarine container because he only had one proper dog dish, and one proper dog. He really wished Jennie would consider taking the pup. The kids would love him, and he wanted to be sure he had a good home.

Maybe he should call her this morning and ask. Before he put the flyers up everywhere.

He wished it had been her tongue he'd felt this morning. He'd woken up with a woodie, and knew that last night he would have given his left nut to sleep with her.

Perhaps it was time he got laid. Found a nice girlfriend. Someone who'd keep him warm this winter. Yes, that's what he'd do. He'd start looking right after the holidays. After Jennie left. His stomach clenched and he felt a pang. Must be indigestion, he figured. He couldn't possibly be feeling anything but lust for the pretty widow. He liked her a lot, but liking and wanting was one thing. It had nothing to do with commitment and love.

He popped an English muffin into the toaster and fried up a slice of ham and an egg. He sat down with his breakfast sandwich and a second hit of coffee and stared out the window at his snow covered lawn.

Sammy laid his head on Nick's foot, and Rasco nipped at his heels. Absently, he broke a little off his sandwich and tossed it under the table. The nipping stopped.

He glanced at his clock over the kitchen sink. It was seven thirty. Too early to call Jennie, he decided. He might as well take his shower and go down to the bistro early. Get his major cooking done for the day. He had several reservations this evening and there were always a lot of drop-ins. The happy hour crowd.

He took a long hot shower but it didn't erase whatever was ailing him. Perhaps he was coming down with a cold or a touch of the flu. He hoped his kissing Jennie last night wouldn't give her whatever bug he'd caught. He wrapped a big towel around himself and then turned the heat up a notch or two. He hated feeling under the weather, but he also knew more was eating him than the common flu.

It was the season to be jolly, and it never failed to make him miserable. The rest of the year he could go about his business and be the guy who had it all— freedom to do what he wanted, a life with few commitments. It was only during the Christmas season that he missed not having a family and the joy it might bring. Might being the key word. It could bring a lot of misery too. He knew that, and had seen it often enough.

Something he avoided at all costs. Look at his mother for instance. What if he ended up being an addict like her? Not that he'd ever do drugs, but maybe it was in his genes. Or worse, he'd transfer that illness on to his kids.

Did he want to take that chance? And he never knew his father. He might have been a drifter, a user himself, and with both of them wasted they'd produced a child. Who knew? Who cared? It didn't define him. He was better than that. Better than a one night stand. Better than a crack-head mother. He was fine just the way he was, and if he sometimes got lonely, well, there were plenty of women willing to help him with that.

An hour later, Nick was in his commercial kitchen at his restaurant cooking up a batch of meatloaf, and his five cheese onion soup. He would also make an herb-crusted pork tenderloin and shrimp scampi over linguini, but that would be done later. Now he just needed to marinate the meat and make the scampi sauce to put in the fridge.

When that was done, he noticed it was almost ten. He hadn't heard from Jennie and wondered if she was still in town. If so he could probably have a quick cup of coffee with her.

He washed his hands, dug out his cell phone and gave her a call. The sound of her voice would ease the pounding in his head and the need to see her. If not, it'd be a weak substitute at best.

She picked up and his pulse kicked in. "Hi, Nick. What's up?"

"Just calling to wish you a good morning," he said, his voice unnaturally husky, "and to let you know how much I enjoyed last night."

"I enjoyed it very much too."

"We should do it again." At her silence, he cleared his throat, and tried for nonchalance. "I was wondering if you were still around? I'm at the bistro, and figured you might pop in for a cup of coffee if you're not too busy."

"I'm in the car right now. On the 95, about fifteen minutes away from Philly. I decided to get the rest of my shopping done. It's easier without the kids around."

"I can understand that." He turned the heat down on one of the burners. "Sorry I missed you."

"Well, I'll see you when I get back. Still haven't heard from Allan, the insurance adjustor. Hopefully he'll let me know tomorrow."

"Right. Well, if you're back here, make sure you call." No mention of Christmas. Maybe she hadn't spoken to her mother yet. She might call him back later with a definite answer. Not that he cared. He could always go to the mall and have dinner at the diner, or accept one of the invitations from one of his lady friends in town. It wasn't like he had no friends. His buddies from high school kept asking him too, but they were married now and lived out west, and he couldn't see going that far for a couple of days. Danny lived in San Francisco and Mark owned a ski shop in Denver. That might be fun if it weren't so far away.

The two single women in town were in their early thirties. One was a nurse, the other worked in the hair salon and gave him great cuts. They both made it plain that they'd like to spend more time with him, but when he did he always felt as if he let them down. They'd have a nice time together, and when he'd leave in the morning their faces would reek of disappointment. He hated hurting them, but he simply didn't care enough to stay.

"Sure. I'll do that." She hesitated, and then spoke again. "About Christmas. I'm not sure that it's a good idea. You know? The kids might think too much of it. My family too, although I'm not worried about them. But when I told the girls about the park and the carriage ride, Katie asked if we were getting married!" She laughed, the sound terrified rather than amused. "Can you imagine? Whatever would give her that crazy idea?"

"I don't know." He rubbed his jaw, thinking aloud. "I see your problem. The girls might be wanting a daddy."

"Exactly." She seemed relieved that he understood so clearly. And he did—but he didn't. "Perhaps giving them a puppy wouldn't be such a bad idea after all. Because Christmas is bound to get weepy without their father around. It'll be hard on everybody."

"Of course. It's going to be very difficult for you." He cleared his throat, his mind spinning. "I wish I could be there for you, but it's probably not a good idea. This is the first Christmas without him, right?"

"Right."

"Well, a dog is your answer then. That'll put a smile on the kids' faces." He added, "You'd be doing me a huge favor by taking Rasco off my hands."

She laughed again, this time the sound relieved. He wasn't sure how he felt about that. "That's what you named him? It's perfect."

"If you want him, you could take him tomorrow or Tuesday, when you come back in town."

"I'll do that, providing no one has claimed him."

"Good. That's a deal then."

"Yes. And thanks for being so understanding about Christmas. I wish I could invite you, I really do."

"That's all right. I know people I can spend the day with."

"I'm sure you do." Her voice had turned cool.

His antenna picked up. Could she be jealous at the idea of him with another woman? Why, hell yes! She just might be. And why did he have to feel so damn good about it?

"If the adjustor can't make it here before Christmas I could bring Rasco to you. Meet you somewhere." He thought quickly, not wanting to show up on her doorstep. "Like a pet store. You'll need a crate, a bed, all that paraphernalia."

"That's true. But even better if I pick all that up now. I'll just hide it in my parent's garage."

"Well, keep in touch. One way or the other we'll get the dog to you."

"Unless someone claims him. He must belong to somebody."

"I haven't seen or heard about anyone looking."

"Put a few flyers up. I'd hate to take him and then have to give him back. That would break the girls' heart."

"We won't let that happen. Trust me, Jennie. I'll make sure the dog is unclaimed before I pass him over to you."

"Thank you." She didn't say anything for a full second. "For everything. I wish things could be different," she whispered.

"So do I." He hung up before his tongue got him into trouble. He didn't even know what he wanted, or what he felt. He had feelings for her, and it had been a long time since he'd been as turned on as last night, but the truth was he had no time for a woman. Between fixing up the farm house and running the bistro his hands were full. Unfortunately, his bed was also empty.

CHAPTER THIRTEEN

Jennie Googled a mall on the outskirts of Philly, eager to find one just off the 95. Before she got out of the car, she wrote down a list of items to buy. Having a game plan made all the difference. She could shop faster and cheaper, and with kids that was just plain smart.

She'd shipped most of the presents by Amazon, but needed a few Santa gifts. During her drive from Norfolk, she'd made a last minute decision to buy her parents a flat screen TV. The one they had now was over ten years old with outdated technology. She wanted to surprise them with something they would use and love.

She entered a Super Wal-Mart store, figuring they'd have pet supplies, toys, and a good-sized electronics department. It took Jennie very little time to pick out a TV for her parents. It would be delivered on the 24th and hooked up for a small extra charge. She found everything she needed for Rasco, and added some chew toys, hoping he might be content with that instead of eating everyone's shoes.

Next, she tossed in some new games the girls would love, a few books to keep them reading during the holidays, and new snowsuits—they'd outgrown theirs from the previous year. She grabbed a couple of Lego sets for the boy cousins, and then headed for the cashiers. There was at least a dozen open, but the lines were long. As she waited, she caught sight of a dancing, musical Santa a few rows away, and stepped out of line to add that to her cart. The girls would crack up.

Heading back, she spotted soup mugs with a Christmas scene that reminded her so much of Heaven, she bought two sets. If she had a chance she'd give one to Nick and keep one for herself. In some minute way it would connect them, and keep his memory alive. Heart humming, she returned to the ever-growing line, feeling proud of her selections and the fact she'd managed to keep within budget.

When she arrived at her parent's she had her father meet her in the garage, and he helped to unload the gifts and put them out of sight. He had some good color in his face and was looking happy and healthy. Perhaps seeing the kids had added exuberance to his step. She certainly hoped so, for he'd be seeing a lot more of them.

Then she entered the home from the garage and the kids came flying into her arms.

"Mommy, Mommy, we had our pictures taken with Santa Claus. He knew we were visiting Nana and Papa, and said he'd make sure the toys came here! How does he know these things, I wonder?" Katie was a very clever girl, and she folded her arms. "I bet you sent him a letter, didn't you? To the North Pole. I wish you had let me write something too."

"You both wrote him a letter a long time ago," Jennie reminded her daughter. "I dropped it off at the mailbox."

"I remember," Brooke said. "I asked him for a piggy. A little one."

Jennie smiled. "And I told you we didn't have any room in our house for a small pig. That's when I suggested a dog. Which you will get when we get our new house," she added, keeping Rasco a secret.

"I know. But what if Santa brings me a pig after all? He might know that I have a collection of pigs on my bed."

"Then I guess we'd have to find a big crate and keep him. But I don't think he'd want to be crated, do you? I can't imagine having a little pig running around our new home, snorting everywhere," she said with a laugh to take any sting out of the words.

Katie pretended to be a pig, running around the living room and snorting. "I'm Miss Piggy," she said, and snorted again.

"That's not funny." Brooke pouted, tears coming to her eyes.

Jennie grabbed her and swung her around. "I love you, sweetheart, and so does Santa. You will have a wonderful Christmas. I promise."

"Okay, Mommy. Nana's making us some lunch. Papa's hungry. And she has some Christmas cookies too. She said we could eat them after lunch. I'm having chicken noodle soup. Nana said she made it from scratch. What's scratch?"

"That's something your mom doesn't do. At least not anymore. It doesn't come out of a can, but is made with all fresh ingredients, like a chicken, and vegetables, and noodles." Jennie shook her head. "Takes a lot of time compared to opening a can. But it's very healthy and good."

"Will I like it?" Katie asked.

Nana heard the remark. "You will love it. It's Papa's favorite too. And I have a loaf of fresh whole grain bread, and cookies or mincemeat tarts for dessert."

"Sounds wonderful, Mom." Jennie kissed her mother's cheek. "What can I do to help?"

"Set the table and put the girl's milk on the table." She looked at her grandchildren. "Have you washed your hands?" she asked.

"Yup," Brooke said, smiling. "This morning after I ate blueberry pancakes and whipping cream."

"In that case it's time for you to do it again."

The girls ran off to wash up, and Jennie poured the milk and sliced the bread.

"So how was the carriage ride through the park last night," her mother asked quietly, shooting a glance at her husband reading in his chair.

"Magical." Jennie paused and looked at her mom, her insides warm as she remembered the feel of Nick's arm around her shoulders. "That's the only word to describe it."

"I like magical," Louise said. "So did anything nice happen during the ride?"

"Nice?" Jennie bristled, upset with herself for being disappointed. "Like how? Everything was wonderful. He's a nice guy, who has no interest in a ready-made family. He's renovating his grandparent's home to get ready for sale, and just bought this business a couple of years ago. He's not looking for a relationship, Mom, if that's what you're hoping to hear." How she wished it was different.

"It is, and you might be wrong." Her mom slipped an arm around her waist and gave her a quick hug. "I saw the way he looked at you. And that man is interested, or I need glasses."

"You might need cataract surgery, not glasses," Jennie said with a chuckle. "He's a man. Men look. They sometimes get tempted even when they know it's not good for them."

"And you? Were you tempted?"

"A little." She glanced around, looking for something else to do. Something that didn't require this line of questioning or meeting her mother's eyes, head on.

"Just a little?"

"He kissed me, okay?" She tossed some napkins on the table and grabbed a large ladle to dish out the soup. "No big deal."

Her mother brushed up beside her and forced Jennie to look her way. "You kissed him? How was it?"

"I didn't say that. It was the other way around. And it was okay."

"Just okay?"

"Okay—a little better than okay."

Her mom beamed. "I'm so glad. I like him, and he likes the children too."

"What are you two whispering about in there?" Her dad got up and opened the fridge door. "I hope you're minding your own business, Louise. Jennie's a grown up woman now, and she doesn't need to tell you everything."

"Jennie's my daughter, and will be until the day I die," her mom huffed. "So yes, she does."

Her dad poured himself a sweetened ice tea and sat at his usual spot, the head of the kitchen table. He winked at Jennie, and she patted his frail shoulder.

"You're right, Dad. A woman my age needs to have some secrets. Not that I have any, or they'd be interesting if I did."

"Then it's high time you made some," her mom said, passing out the soup bowls.

The girls took their seats, and because it was a special occasion to have family around, Katie said Grace, adding how thankful she was to be at Nana's and Papa's. That earned her hugs and smiles, and the discussion about Nick was put on hold.

Funny thing was, even though they weren't talking about him she wished he could be here. He would like her parents, and they already liked him. But it would be much too easy to let her emotions go. She was vulnerable right now, not having a man to hold her at night, someone to curl up with and talk to. It was lonely, and it might not go away anytime soon, but she couldn't replace Daniel. Not yet.

The soup and bread were delicious and even the girls lapped it up. Jennie removed the bowls and put the plate of cookies on the table. "So, Mom, Dad. It may take several months before our house sells, but I'd just like to get an idea of neighborhoods and pricing around here. Is there a real estate paper that I can look at, or Dad, would you like to go for a drive?"

"Mommy? We're supposed to make snowmen this afternoon." Katie folded her arms and gave her a determined look. "We missed you, and want you to play with us."

"You're right, sweetheart," Jennie said, realizing that it was vacation. A holiday. Her plans for a new life would have to wait. "We can think about the move another time. After Christmas. Now is Santa time, and thinking about what he will bring my little girls, and spending time with Nana and Papa."

"And making snowmen," Katie added firmly.

Busted. She would have to go out in the cold with the kids, instead of sitting by the warmth of the fire. When had she gotten old? Only a year or two ago she'd have loved to frolic in the snow, tossing snowballs, chasing the girls, making angels and snowmen, and running inside for carrots for their nose. Life had been fun. But she knew the answer to her question. That had ended the day she heard Daniel's helicopter had gone down.

"Christy's bringing the boys over in an hour." Her mother offered Papa a mincemeat tart, knowing it was one of his favorite holiday treats. "They want to see the girls and I thought it would be nice for you and Christy to catch up too."

"Great, Mom. I'm glad they're all coming. Is Matt joining us?"

"I'm not sure. He might. He likes to sit and watch football with your dad."

"And drink my beer," John mumbled good-naturedly. "Good thing they only live two miles away." He glanced at Jennie. "That's a mighty fine neighborhood."

When her sister's family showed up, the girls and Jennie were already rolling in the snow, having snowball fights and seeing who could make the best angel.

The boys piled out and ran toward the girls, jumping in the snow, and knocking Brooke down in the process. Jennie waited to see what happened and sighed with relief when her daughter squealed with delight.

Christy jumped out of the new Lexus SUV, reached down for some snow and tossed a big fluffy snowball right at her. Jennie dodged the one in the face, and picked up her own ball and ran toward her sister. She tossed it just at the right time, and then the fight was on. Laughing they both grappled in the snow like they were children again, determined to outdo the other. Her sister was two years younger, but Jennie was feisty and didn't like to lose. Especially in a snowball fight. The children got in the act, and soon it was a free-for-all.

It ended when one of the kids got Matt—carrying in bags of presents—smack in the face.

"That's enough," he snapped. "Boys. Help me unload the car."

"Okay, Dad." Heads down Jed and Jake returned to the car and dragged out more bags filled with presents.

The girls stopped to watch. "Look!" Brooke shouted, dancing around the boys. "Can I see? Is one for me?"

"Naw," Jake, the older boy said. "We didn't get you anything."

Brooke's face fell, and Jennie could see she was about to cry. "Don't tease her. I'm sure there is more than one for each of my girls."

Before he could say anything, Christy grabbed one of the big bags out of Jake's hands. "Why, I think I see one in here for Brooke, and another for Katie. But none for bad boys," she added with a grin.

"I'm good most of the time," Jake answered, checking the name tags on the gifts.

Her mom and dad had the front door open. "I swear, you boys are getting bigger every time I see you," their Papa said, giving each boy a hug.

"You always say that," Jed said, kissing his Nana. "We just saw you last week."

"And you look like you've grown an inch since then too," Louise said playing along. "Must be the Christmas cookies I sent home with you."

"Here, let us take those." John took the bags out of their hands. When the last of the presents were inside, he directed the kids to the garage. They knew the routine. Once they hit the mudroom, they peeled off their boots and outer clothing before being allowed indoors.

They came in, four little bodies, full of laughter, mischief, and fun. Jennie could see the happiness on her daughters' faces, and stopped worrying about the boys teasing and rough play. The girls loved their big cousins, and were loved back. And when it came to family, that was all that mattered.

Nick's face flashed to mind. He would be alone for Christmas. And even with all her family around, so would she. If only there was someway they could be together without arousing her children's or her mother's hopes. Or her own.

CHAPTER FOURTEEN

Nick got his cooking done, then remembered his promise to Jennie about posting the Lost Dog flyers he'd printed out. He was surprised by his reluctance to do so—but he didn't want to hand the mutt over to just anybody. Anybody but Jennie, that is.

What if the dog did belong to somebody? After all, a pup like that didn't just materialize out of the blue. He might not be a pedigree, but he looked to be part Dalmatian and was about as cute as puppies get. Truthfully, he half hoped that some passerby had dropped him off in Heaven because they couldn't take care of the animal.

It had occurred to him that if someone claimed Rasco, Jennie would have to find another pup for the girls, and he wouldn't have an excuse to see her again. That could explain some of his reluctance, but why was he feeling so let down just because she uninvited him for Christmas? He didn't blame her. Christmas was for loved ones and families, or charity cases. He was neither. He didn't need a hand out or a meal, and he didn't need to be taken in like some stray.

Maybe he should invite Byron and Ally over to his place this year. They could have their own turkey dinner, and then enjoy some eggnog in front of the fire.

That was a hellova an idea. And he should pick up a present for them too. Strolling down Main Street, he put up his flyers and glanced in store windows. What would a photographer like, he wondered. Buying her a camera seemed a little over the top, but maybe she'd like some real good quality frames. That was impersonal enough, but appropriate. Byron was always sprouting off poetry as if he thought he was the real deal. A book of poems seemed kind of lame. What would a young, randy man want for a present that he didn't already have? A gag bag maybe, stuffed with poetry books and a box of condoms. That might get a few laughs.

He was smiling now as he went into a little bookstore and found the small shelf of poetry. He had no idea what Byron already owned, and in a town like this his choice would be limited. Maybe he read with an ereader, and downloaded his books from the internet. Hell if he knew.

He walked up to the middle-aged clerk, a man around fifty, with an equally big girth. "Hi. I've never been in your store before, I'm sorry to say. I'm Nick. Own the bistro up the street."

"Sure, I've seen you around. I'm Roger," he offered his hand. "How can I help you? If you want something in particular I can order it. Guaranteed before Christmas."

"That soon?" Nick shook his head. "Not sure. Do you know Byron Watts? He works for me. Likes poetry."

"I sure do. He likes to browse for the classics. Once in awhile he picks up some kids books. And he's big on Fantasy. You buying something for him?"

"Yeah, but I don't know much about his taste." Nick stuffed his hands in his back pockets. Fantasy? What did that even mean? "Can you guide me here?"

"Sure thing. I think his children books are for family members, but I know he likes sci-fi, or Lord of the Rings stuff."

He never would have pegged Byron as a Tolkien buff. "Is there anything new out?"

"Yeah. A collector's edition for the holiday."

"I'll take it." When his gift was bought and wrapped up, Nick entered a hobby store that had a large selection of frames. Picked a few to match the woodsy photos Ally took. Then he returned to work in time for lunch.

Ally came in first. "Hey, boss. How're you doing?"

"Fine. I was putting up lost and found posters for that pup I'd been chasing, and I got to thinking. How would you and Byron like to come over Christmas day? Have dinner. A few drinks and laughs."

She eyed him with curiosity. "Geez, that would be great, but I already have plans." Ally touched his arm. "What about you? Don't you have any family nearby?"

"No, no family." He shrugged as if that was the last thing he needed. "Anyway, I'm glad you have plans, figured you might be on your own."

Byron walked in. "Plans for what," he asked, removing his wool cap.

"For Christmas. Nick wants to invite you and me."

130

Byron raised a brow. "Sorry, boss, but I'm busy too." He stepped around the bar and hitched his ass on a stool. "Why the invite? Don't you have anywhere to go?"

Nick felt his cheeks grow warm, and his spine stiffened. "Sure, but I decided to have guests over instead. Thought you guys might be on your own, and wanted to include you in the festivities. But if you're both busy, well, no worries."

"Festivities, huh?" Byron chuckled. "Sure sounds like fun, but I'll be out of town for a night or two."

"Just a few people over. Not exactly festive," he mumbled. He didn't know why he lied, but it seemed so dismally lame not to have family or friends or any loved ones to spend the holiday with. Even his two drifter employees had plans.

Maybe it was time for Nick to get a life.

* * *

They only had four tables of diners in for lunch, and closed early. Nick was locking away the cash when his cell phone rang and he saw it was Jennie calling.

Like an idiot his heartbeat speeded up, and he damn near smiled. What was he? A schoolboy with a crush? Why was he behaving like some pimply jerk-face who'd never been laid? Probably had a lot to do with Christmas, and the letdown feeling that always accompanied it. He didn't really *hate* Christmas, he just didn't like it very much. Let's just say, he preferred the rest of the year.

Heck, even Valentine's Day was friendlier, with far less stress. He had a wonderful Valentine's last year. Took his date into Philly and they stayed at the Hyatt. They went dining and dancing at a hot new nightspot, and she'd been thrilled. They both drank a little too much champagne and then went back to their room and tumbled in bed. Had a hellova time too.

There wasn't anything wrong with him—or his equipment. Both were in fine working order. He enjoyed female company, especially in bed, as much as the next guy, but he also liked his free time too. Being a bachelor had some perks. He could be with a girl when he wanted to, but if he wanted to go hiking in the woods, or climbing Mount Kilimanjaro, well he could do that too. Without asking permission.

And he didn't have to buy the cow to sample the milk, although that wasn't really what it was about. He just didn't get off on dating a lot of women and banging a new one every week. That was Byron's forte. One day he hoped to find a woman of his own, one that he looked forward to waking up to, and saying goodnight as their heads hit the pillow. A companion, a friend, lover and wife. He wanted that very much.

He might need to move that off the back burner and put it up front on simmer.

All those thoughts went in and out of his head as he answered the call. "Jennie. How's it going?"

"Great! Can't you hear by all the noise behind me? My nephews are over. Everybody has new Lego sets and they're squabbling over the pieces." She laughed. "I'm calling because I heard from Allan. You know—the insurance adjustor. He wants to meet me tomorrow at eleven. I know you'll probably be busy cooking right about then, but if possible I'd like to pick up what we talked about. If it's not taken."

"I haven't been home to answer the phone or check my emails, but nobody has called my cell or come to the restaurant to claim him."

"That's good, but if anything changes, please call me at once. I'd need to get busy on it, if you know what I mean."

"I do. Of course, I'll call. Can you get away early? Meet me at the house around eight thirty or nine? We can do it then, or after the lunch hour crowd leaves. We closed today around two."

"After would work best for me."

He could hear the children arguing in the background. "Sounds like you've got a hundred kids over."

"Nope. That's just four. How can some people have a dozen children?" she asked and laughed again.

"Beats me. Two dogs are enough."

There was silence on the other end of the phone, and he regretted his words, wishing he could slip them back. "I mean one day I want kids. Just not right now." *Shit!* He'd just made it worse.

"I understand." Her voice was cool, crisp, like a winter fog.

"I didn't exactly mean that. I'm envious of people who have a good family life. I never had that myself."

"That is sad. I'm sorry. So what are you going to do for Christmas? You can't be alone."

"I invited Byron and Ally over. They're going to let me know." Another lie. He was an honest person, but he didn't want anyone to think he was pitiful. He'd rather be a liar than someone to be pitied.

"I hope it works out, for all of you." He heard her mother's voice in the background asking if it was Nick she was talking to. "Invite him for Christmas," he heard her mother say.

"I've got to go, Nick," she said hurriedly. "I'll see you tomorrow."

"Have a good night." He turned his phone off and jammed it in his pant pocket, grabbed his coat, and locked up. He'd go home for a few hours, maybe get his little black book out and see who was still available.

Being a single woman and a nurse, Linda probably already signed up to work. Jordon, his hair stylist, might still be free. Perhaps he could do something nice for her. Take her into Philly. They could go see the Nutcracker. He wasn't a fan of ballet, but it was supposed to be a beautiful show. They could spend the night, have sex and a very nice Christmas.

He'd call her right away before he had a chance to change his mind. Her number was on his cell. He'd check in. They usually got together every few months.

She answered on the first ring. "Hey, Nick. How're you doing? Surviving the holidays?"

"Yeah. Barely. I was just checking to see if you were free. Thought we might go into Philly Christmas morning. Spend the day and catch a show that night. It would be fun."

"Uh, sorry, Nick, but you're about two months out of date." She hesitated. "I'm seeing someone. A chiropractor."

"Oh! Well." He frowned. Why hadn't he known? He'd been in for a haircut ten days ago. She hadn't said anything about it. Feeling foolish, he said, "I'm happy for you. Hope everything works out and that he's good to you."

"So far, things are looking up." Jordon added casually, "Try Linda. She's been seeing a young intern lately, but you never know."

His jaw dropped. They knew about each other? Damn. His reputation wasn't much better than Byron. Time to make a few changes around here.

CHAPTER FIFTEEN

Jennie commandeered the upstairs bathroom early the next morning. She wanted to get her hair washed and her legs shaved before the girls got up and demanded her attention. She'd be wearing jeans, so shaving was optional as no one would be seeing her legs, but it made her feel attractive.

And just because the girls and her family needed distancing from Nick, didn't mean she had to stay clear. Protecting her daughters was her priority. Not maintaining celibacy. So just in case, she gave herself a really good shave, put on soothing body lotion to fight off the harsh winter dryness, and a touch of perfume on the nape of her neck.

Not that she was planning on doing anything with Nick, and she hadn't even met the insurance adjustor yet, but preparation never hurt anyone.

Jennie dried her hair, trying to eliminate the frizz and curl, and it fell sleek and pretty to her shoulders. Her green eyes sparkled and she wondered if it was all the thoughts running through her head.

She had the good girl inside warring with the naughty one. Good girl says, get out of Heaven as quickly as possible. Make the necessary arrangements for the car, pick up Rasco, smile nicely at Nick and wish him a very happy Christmas. Good girl says it wouldn't be bad to give him a friendly kiss on the cheek.

Bad girl says that's a terrible idea. She had a perfect opportunity to have great sex for the first time in a year. No one other than her, Nick and the dog would ever know. He would like it, she would like it, and then she could return to her children and her family bright-eyed and bushy-tailed. It would be a very jolly Christmas indeed.

Bad girl smiled at herself in the mirror. Jennie turned her back on her, and walked into the bedroom to quickly get dressed. The girls were up, she could hear them giggling in the bedroom next door. They had twin beds, and Nana had put up a small Christmas tree for them. They were beyond excited about Santa coming, and so far, they had yet to mention their dad.

It made her sad, for she was a good girl after all. Her kids were adjusting to life without Daniel. Their tears had stopped and they didn't keep asking for him. But she wanted to keep his memory alive, and forgetting that wonderful man and father would be a tragedy.

She slipped into a light blue pair of undies and a matching bra. Her breasts were good and even after two children her stomach was firm and flat. Weight had never been an issue, but her appetite had waned significantly in the past year. There were nights when she and the kids ate Healthy Choice dinners and light popcorn for dessert.

Those nights were increasing lately, although she made a point to always cook a proper meal for the three of them on weekends.

Once she was dressed in her jeans and a long sleeved mint green tee, she popped her head into the girls' room. "What's going on in here?" she whispered, not hearing anyone stirring downstairs. She stepped inside and gave them both a kiss. "Have I told you lately that I love you?"

"Uh-huh. When you said goodnight," Brooke answered.

"And yesterday morning when we jumped in your arms," Katie said laughing. She tossed a pillow at her mother. "Can we have another snowball fight?"

"Yeah!" Brooke jumped out of her own bed, and pounced on her sister. "Can we? Please?"

"Well, I would love to say yes, but I have to go and speak to the adjustor about my car. If you like I could drop you off at Aunt Christy's or leave you here with Nana and Papa."

"Uh. I want to do both," Brooke said. "What do you want to do Katie?"

"I want to go ice skating. Can we come with you, Mom? Can we?"

She would have said yes, but for the dog. "I'm not sure how long the car's going to take. It wouldn't be any fun for you kids waiting around in a gas station. "Maybe Aunt Christy will take you and the boys skating."

"I think she will," Brooke said, with a determined tilt to her chin. "Call and ask her, pretty please?"

"I'll do that." Jennie kissed her tiny nose. "And when I get back we'll go see the tree lights in the neighborhood.

That's always fun. And don't forget we have tickets to Disney on Ice for Boxing day."

"When is Christmas again?" Brooke asked.

Katie answered, "Two more days. It's Monday, and Christmas is Wednesday. Then we go to Disney on Ice the following day. Right, Mom?"

"That's right, and we still have more days before we have to drive home. We will leave here on New Year's Day."

"When is that?" Brooke wanted to know.

"A week from Christmas, so it's a Wednesday."

"Okay. I have to go to the bathroom now." Jennie smiled as Brooke trotted off. "She's an amazing little girl, just like you are. I'm a lucky ducky having you both."

"I miss Dad," Katie said and buried her head in the pillow. "Every single day."

"I do too, sweetheart. But he's not far away. He's in the clouds and can hear you and see you, and knows when you're thinking about him. He knows when you're happy and sad, and it's okay to talk to him. I do all the time."

"Santa knows when we're happy and sad too. Maybe he lives near Santa. Heaven's beyond the clouds, probably not far from the North Pole."

Jennie gave up on that logic and kissed her daughter's head. "You're probably right. Maybe he's helping Santa with the gifts this year, and he'll get an extra special one for you and Brooke."

Katie sat up, her auburn braids on either side of her face. Her brown eyes widened as she grinned. "That's way cool."

"You're way cool. Now how about you go to the bathroom and then get dressed? I'll be down in the kitchen."

"Okay, Mom. If you see Nick, tell him we hope he has a happy Christmas."

"I will my love." Smiling, she left her daughters to dress, and went downstairs to make the coffee and get the children's breakfast started.

She called her sister, and Christie said she'd be happy to take the kids to the rink. "When we're done I'll drop them back at Grandma's. So, tell me, is this trip to Heaven all business, or will you be mixing in a little pleasure?"

"Uh, not sure what you mean. But yes, I will deal with the car and then pick up a surprise for the girls."

"The dog that you almost ran over?"

"That's the one. Unless someone claimed him."

"I think they would have by now. But it is strange, isn't it?"

"I guess so. If they didn't want him, why not put him in a shelter?" Jennie lowered her voice, not wanting the girls to hear what they were talking about. "Maybe he ran away and got lost."

"Or was sent by an angel."

"Yeah." Jennie glared at the phone. "Like that's real likely."

"So are you going to see Mr. Chef and Good looking?"

She laughed. "Yes."

"Well, in that case, have fun. Don't rush back. I'll take care of the girls."

"I'm not staying the night," Jennie said sharply. "I'm not at all ready for that."

"You've got to do it sometime, hon. Might as well take the plunge."

"It will happen when the time is right. If it's this afternoon, so be it."

"Did you shave your legs?" Christy asked.

"Of course."

Her sister giggled. "So, it did cross your mind. Remember we always said if you don't shave, you won't be tempted. That was our no-sex rule."

As if she'd forgotten? "Just a precaution." She cleared her throat. "I can't imagine what it will feel like. You know? Someone new?"

"It will feel wonderful, and exciting, and all those good things."

"Gotta go, Chris. I hear the pitter-patter of little feet coming down the stairs."

"Tell the girls I'll pick them up at ten."

"Thanks, sis."

"Go. Do it! This could be your Christmas present to yourself. You deserve it, honey."

The words stayed with her during the short ride to Heaven. She wasn't sure what she deserved anymore. Everything she'd ever wanted had been hers, and then it was taken away. What would an afternoon of sex prove? That she wasn't dead from the waist down? The kiss had told her that. She'd felt a tingling and a need, and even though she felt guilty about it, she wanted to do it again. She wanted to feel. To love. Was that so wrong? It seemed like a betrayal to Daniel and yet, when will she have mourned long enough? One year, two years, a decade from now?

CHAPTER SIXTEEN

A light snow was falling by the time she entered Heaven. Just as it had the day she had hit the tree. And met Nick. It was a soft, fluffy snow, not the kind that made driving hazardous, but the kind that angels would make, creating a magical holiday mood to lift the spirits. Her heart was lighter already.

There was something so peaceful and serene about this town. A safe harbor for her battered heart and wounded soul. She knew Nick was lonely. Oh, he'd never admit it, but he seemed like a man that had never had many friends. A loner, someone who didn't quite fit in. He was liked by everyone, or so it seemed, but she sensed that he was on guard. On guard for what? What was he afraid of?

Rejection? Falling in love? Being vulnerable? Heck, all people felt that to some extent, but if you didn't open your heart and go for it, then you were living in a vacuum.

When she arrived at the gas station, the adjustor had not yet shown up, so she called Nick to let him know she was in town.

"You're here?" he asked, and she could swear she heard excitement in his voice.

"I am. Just waiting on this guy—again. Guess I have to get an appraisal next."

"That shouldn't be difficult. Once you get past this, things will start moving quickly," he told her. "When do you have to be back in Virginia?"

"Not 'til Monday, the 4th."

"That gives you plenty of time."

"It better," she said with a smile. "So are you at the restaurant cooking?"

"I am. Can't you smell it?"

"Uh, garlic, herbs, butter, am I getting close?"

"Good guess. Not the butter though. I'm making a Sambuca tomato sauce which is amazing over fresh grilled shrimp. The anise flavor of the Sambuca melds beautifully with the richness of fresh tomatoes and basil. Don't you agree?"

She laughed. "Oh, by all means. My mouth is already watering."

"Stay tonight. Come for dinner."

"I can't. I've got to get back to the kids and family."

He was silent for a few moments. "When you finish up with your car, at least join me at the bistro for lunch. Then you can follow me back home, pick up Rasco, and leave whenever you're ready. Although I do believe another ride in the park might be in order."

Her pulse speeded up and she swallowed hard, thinking about that first kiss, followed by the others. Nothing clumsy or intrusive, as if he was careful and considerate about her feelings. She wondered how hot his kisses would be if she wasn't a widow.

"I see a car pulling up," she said, sounding breathless. "I better go."

"Fine. I'll be waiting for you."

She felt a sexual stirring in her tummy. Was she making too much out of nothing? One more desperate woman who wanted to snag this great guy?

"Later," she said and hung up, then left the warm interior of her rented car to meet the gentleman heading her way.

"Thank you for coming so soon," she said, offering her hand. "I wasn't sure if I'd see you before Christmas."

"I'm working until four tomorrow, then I can enjoy the holiday." He gave her a brief smile and shook her hand. "This won't take long. Let's have a look and then you can be on your way."

Jennie grabbed a coffee from the shop, and said hello to Geoff who was working the morning shift. She scanned a local paper and before she was through the adjustor was done. He asked her some questions, took down her information, and said they would be in touch.

It wasn't even noon, but she was free to leave. Knowing Main Street had no parking she left her rental car where it was and walked the short distance. Snow fell, but it wasn't cold. She felt blanketed in peace.

She popped into a few of the gift stores and even bought herself a book to read. She figured she'd take it with her to the bistro, and have something to get herself immersed in while Nick was busy with the lunch crowd.

When she entered, Ally gave her a big smile and pointed to the kitchen door. "He's waiting in there. Has a table set up just for you." Her eyes were twinkling. "What did you do to this guy? He's never been so ga-ga over anyone before. Not since I've known him anyway."

Jennie's knees wobbled. Her insides were jumping all over the place. Could this be real? Did she want Nick to care about her? Was she ready to care about him?

"I think he just feels responsible," she said slowly. "He thinks the car crash ruined my holidays."

"It's more than that. A little guilt, maybe. But he's been in and out of the restaurant for the past half hour, looking for you. Told me he wanted to serve you himself. Then he put a table together, found a tablecloth, and asked Byron to run down the street and get some flowers." Ally's eyes were big, her smile wide. "He's gone overboard to impress you."

Jennie's heart hummed. Was he the one who'd make her heart kick start again? Could these feelings be strong enough to survive the winter months, the distance between them, and did she want them to be? Her pulse raced with excitement, and a touch of fear. She knew nothing of what the future would bring. It was just the here and now.

"I like him too," she said simply and pushed the kitchen door open to step inside.

Nick's face lit up, and her own face split into a smile. She felt young, beautiful and wanted. "Hey," she said softly, moving forward. "You've been looking for me?"

"I have." He reached for her hands and pulled her to his chest. His mouth came down on hers. Firm. In control. Letting her know exactly what he wanted, and how much he needed. He kissed her for several seconds, and they both heard the kitchen door open, and then close again. He still didn't release her.

Finally she broke away, her eyes searching his face, seeing more than she was ready for. "I missed you," he said.

"Nick..." she began.

"I know. It's too soon. But I'm a patient man."

She bit her bottom lip, wondering exactly how patient. "I'll be going back to Virginia for the school term. I'm not taking the kids out in the middle of the year. I'll be gone in a week."

"I know. That's fine. But I have today. At least a few hours, so let me enjoy it." He pulled out a folding chair from the makeshift table, and she sat with a wide smile. Anise, garlic, wine. If this wasn't heaven, it sure was temptation.

"This is so sweet of you."

"I thought you might want to sample that shrimp dish, and it's not being served until tonight. It's this evening's special."

"I would." She fiddled with her napkin, embarrassed by his show of affection. "Thank you."

He poured her a glass of Chardonnay. She saw the label and recognized it as a very highly priced wine.

She lifted her glass. "Won't you have one too?"

His eyes brightened. "I will. Why not? We're celebrating the holidays."

"Do you ever skip work? What happens if you're not here?"

"Ally and Byron cover for me."

"I see." After he poured his own glass, she raised hers in a toast. "Maybe we could celebrate early?" Her heart fluttered. How could she have just said that? Did she really want to sleep with him? Her body was crying with need, but what about her heart? What if after he took the night off, she couldn't go through with it?

He clinked glasses with her, his eyes never leaving her face. "That's the best idea I've heard in years."

She took a sip of the delicious wine and then set her glass down. He did also, copying her movements. He captured her face in his hands and bent to give her a soft, gentle kiss that stirred her insides and warmed her soul. She felt herself melt, wanting to believe that he might be the one. Someone to end her heartache, someone to love.

"This is happening so soon. I don't know what to think," she said, fighting the urge to run like the wind, or hang on tight and never let him go.

"I don't either. Let's not worry about it." He straightened and put a hand on her shoulder, giving it a squeeze. "See what happens."

He turned away, and she felt cold. She wanted his hands on her, his kisses, and more. She watched his back for a moment, trying to make sense of it all, but it was an impossible task. She'd only met him a few days ago, whatever they were feeling had to be lust. Not love. Intelligently, she knew that, but her heart wouldn't accept it.

When he turned he had a plate in his hands. The shrimp with the Sambuca sauce sat atop a small serving of angel hair pasta. A single purple flower adorned the plate, and a small vase with more cut flowers sat on the table. His thoughtfulness and care meant so much to her that she blinked back tears.

"You inspired me this morning," he said, sliding the plate in front of her. Then he broke a stem from one of the cut flowers and put it behind her ear. "Let me know what you think."

She lifted her fork and brought a shrimp to her mouth. It was hot. She blew on it, her eyes on his. Then she bit into the deliciously flavored shrimp, and nearly simpered with pleasure. A man who could cook like this was worth his weight in gold. "This dish tastes like heaven." She smiled. "No wonder you opened your bistro here. Nowhere else would have been good enough."

He was busy for the next half hour as two tables came in and he had to fill their orders. But it was fun to sit in the kitchen with him, sipping her wine, and watching the man work. It was obvious that he loved what he did. Perhaps he was showing off a little, but he certainly had flare. Slicing and dicing with a sharp silver knife—flipping vegetables and beef in a skillet without the use of a spatula. She wondered how he could do that. The oil would have splattered her and the stove, but not so with him.

He was a man with skills, and she made the decision to learn what else he did well.

CHAPTER SEVENTEEN

By the time Nick closed up and they drove to his home it was nearly three. He had told Ally he wouldn't be returning tonight, but that everything was ready and all she needed was to warm the food, put it on a plate, and she'd be good to go.

Ally had given her a look, surprised and a little wary. It was obvious that she cared about her boss, and didn't want to see him hurt.

They left her car at the garage as after two glasses of wine, she had a slight buzz. Walking to his Jeep, she tucked her hand under his arm, feeling as though she were floating on air. The idea of making love to this delicious man was tantalizing. For the past two hours she'd watched him work, seeing the numerous things those hands could do. She wanted to feel them on her so much that even in the chilly air she was burning up.

The whole set-up at the restaurant—a table for two, flowers, wine, lingering glances and tiny kisses between dishes—had been an act of seduction. Foreplay. And oh God, did it work. They couldn't get there soon enough.

She crossed her legs in the Jeep and folded her arms. Snuck glances at his strong profile. His face was set in stone, his hands on the wheel slightly unsteady. She had the feeling that he was feeling the heat of the moment too.

He shot her a look that burned deep. "You okay?"

"Uh...yeah. You?"

"I feel like a teenager ready to explode. I want you so bad, I can hardly drive."

She glanced down and saw the tightness in his jeans. She laughed, and touched his thigh. "How much further?"

"Five more minutes."

"Hurry, please hurry." She licked her lips and slid her hand up and down his leg. "This is crazy. But I'm not afraid. I want to do this. With you."

He understood. "I promise you won't regret it. And if you change your mind, we can stop at any time."

"I won't change my mind." She took her hand off his leg and settled back in the car, trying not to think of Daniel or what this moment would mean. It didn't lesson her love for her husband, and never would. It only meant that she might be ready to love again.

As soon as they were parked, she flung the door open and ran around for a kiss. She was half afraid that they might lose this connection if she allowed her head to get involved. And she didn't want that to happen. The next few hours belonged to her. And Nick. The rest of the world could just darn well wait.

His tongue slid into her mouth and mingled with her own. His breath tasted sweet, like the mocha latte they had drank together after their meal. She stood on tiptoe to get a little more of him, and his hands slipped inside her open jacket. They found her breasts, and even through the tee shirt her nipples tightened, aching for his touch.

So good. So right. "Let's get inside," she said, not recognizing her own voice.

"Mind the dogs," he said, opening the door, and ushering her in, while his leg fought the large dog and a smaller one from jumping all over her.

She laughed, and stooped to pet the two of them, giving them both a hug and kiss.

He watched her for a minute, then he pulled her up and into his arms.

"Save those for me." He slid her jacket off her shoulders and tossed it onto a bench. He removed his own, and kicked off his boots. She stepped out of hers.

His arms went around her middle drawing her near. Her breath hitched in her throat. His thighs were pressed against hers, and she felt his bulge. Her blood skyrocketed, and she moved her hips to feel him better. Had anything ever been quite this good?

One hand drifted down to her ass, and pulled her in closer. She shifted her weight and widened her stance, making room for him. He fit himself between her legs, and she hung on to his shoulders, head thrown back, allowing one sensation after another to sweep over her body. He kissed her neck, and nibbled his way to her ear. He swept it with his tongue, and then kissed his way back down again. His hand was massaging her ass, and he was moving ever so slowly against her, building a friction between them that would ignite too quickly, if he didn't stop soon.

"Nick?"

"Uh-huh?" He was pushing at her t-shirt now. Lifting it up, kissing her tummy, until his mouth latched onto her nipple, and he sucked it through the lacy material of her bra.

She cried out.

He didn't release, but sucked harder. She moved her hips against him. Aching. Wanting. Needing.

His hands slid around her back and unhooked her bra. Then he lifted her arms and tossed her bra and tee onto the bench. She was wearing only her jeans, and she felt a moment's shame and tried to cover herself. He didn't let her.

"Don't. Let me look at you." His eyes feasted on her and he groaned. "You are so beautiful. Every part of you." He pulled her into his arms and kissed her deeply, then he used his legs to back-step her inside. They passed the kitchen and then he picked her up and carried her into his bedroom and laid her down.

He flung off his sweater, and laid next to her, taking her back into his arms. They kissed some more, and then he took his mouth away, his lips trailing down to her breasts. He licked both nipples erect, and sucked gently on one, tweaking the other with his fingers. She felt the pressure inside of her building, and held his head and arched her back, offering her breasts for his mouth, his tongue. She ached for him.

His kisses and caresses weren't good enough. She had to feel him too. She broke away, wanting to touch and taste him as he had her. She ran her fingers over his chest, feeling his hard muscles contract. He had broad shoulders and a narrow waist, and didn't look like he ate his own cooking. His chest was solid, with only a light smattering of dark curly hair. She ran her fingers through it. She kissed his nipples, and heard him sigh. Then curiosity got the better of her, and she undid his fly. He was wearing boxer shorts, and she put her hand in, feeling the length of him, enjoying the power it gave her when his cock pulsed in her hand.

She got to her knees and pulled his jeans off him. Next came the shorts. She ran her hands up his long legs, and cupped him.

He cursed and tossed her over, unzipping her pants, and sliding them down her legs. He left her panties on and put his mouth on her. Hot breath and greedy fingers touched her where she wanted it the most. She arched toward him and called out his name.

"Now, Nick. Take me now."

Needing no more encouragement, Nick slipped her undies off, grabbed a condom from the bedside dresser, and slipped it over his erect penis. She watched his movements, wet with need. Straddling her, he bent to kiss her softly, and then ever so gently he pushed inside.

Jennie held on to his shoulders, taking him deep. She had wondered what this moment would be like—would she be filled with regret or shame? Instead, she widened her legs and welcomed him in, happiness nearly ripping her apart. His mouth demanded more and she answered back. His movements became hurried, then gentled. He touched her breasts and she moaned with pleasure. He withdrew a little, enough so that he could slip in a finger to find her sweet spot. Knowing what she needed, what she wanted, he touched her delicate bud, until she buckled with pleasure. Then he pushed himself in deep.

The climax came fast and furious, and she dug her nails into his shoulders, eager for every sensation, wanting it to last and last.

It had been more than a year, and this could be her very own Christmas gift.

CHAPTER EIGHTEEN

After a few minutes, Nick rolled off of her. Breathing heavily, he cradled her head on his shoulder, and kissed her damp forehead. He hoped she was okay. He had meant to be gentle and take it easy, but in the end he couldn't.

She was perhaps the sexiest woman he ever had the pleasure to meet. And God, she was sweet. Passionate, beautiful, and kind and caring, Jennie was a sweetheart, with a lot of love in her still yet to give. He hated the thought of someone else having this woman lying beside him. She was the exact type of person he'd waited his whole life to find. Someone he'd enjoy talking to at the end of each day, someone to kiss hello in the morning.

If only he could convince her to stay.

He dropped a kiss on her shoulder, and she put a hand on his cheek. "That was amazing," she said softly.

His heart yearned. "So were you. I hope you're not regretting anything."

"No. Not at all." She flipped over and was face to face with him. "I do have one regret. I wish I could spend the night with you, but the kids are expecting me home. I should probably leave, and let you get back to work."

He glanced out the window. "It's snowing pretty hard."

She laughed and twisted her head around. "Really? How hard?"

He felt his dick pick up interest. "Hard enough. Just as I will be in a minute." He kissed her nose, and placed her hand on his growing erection. "Just lie here and think about it for awhile." He traced the outline of her breast, and watched her face grow rosy.

She was the prettiest, sweetest woman in the world, and he didn't want to see her go. At least not today. He wasn't a greedy man, and he knew that she had a life and it wasn't in Heaven.

"Stay with me." He kissed her mouth softly, one hand playing with her long strands of hair. "I'll cook you dinner and we can eat it in bed."

"You just fed me lunch."

"Yes, I did, but by the time I get through with you this afternoon, you will be starved, I promise." He kissed her deeply this time, his hand brushing over her nipples with a light touch, knowing they might still be tender.

"You're pretty cock sure of yourself, aren't you?" she said, stroking him the way he'd hoped.

"You keep that up, and we will see." He looked into her eyes, and they were smiling. He had made her happy, and that knowledge settled deep inside of him, making him prouder than he'd ever been.

"I could grow to like you very much." He traced her eyebrows, and kissed her cheek. "I already love your kids. It's you that I'm not so sure about."

She jerked away from him, a puzzled expression on her face. "Why? What's wrong with me?"

"You live too far away. How am I going to do this to you," he touched her between her legs, "if you're all the way in Virginia?"

She gasped, and opened her thighs a little. "Oh. Oh. I see what you mean."

"You do?" He lifted the sheet and dove under. He kissed her softly until she pulled at his hair. He came up for air.

"I'm hungry now."

"Already?" He stroked her, noticing that she was wet, and moving against his hand. "I thought we could stay in bed a little longer."

"What I'm hungry for is you." She pushed out of the bed and ran toward the bathroom. "Just got to clean up a minute. Have you got another one of those condom things?"

He grinned. "I've got a whole box."

"Good. Keep them handy." She closed the door behind her and he laughed. Damn he hadn't felt this good in years. Or ever. Was she the one? It was too soon to say, but they were off to a great start.

She walked out of the bathroom, a hand on her hip, a sexy smile on her face. Her long legs strode confidently over the carpet, and she stood next to the bed looking at him, an inch at a time. Damn that was hot.

She ran her hand threw her tousled hair and when she arched her back he almost cried. This was like a strip tease, without any clothes. "You see anything you like?" she asked in a husky voice.

"Get over here, you sexy witch." He grabbed her hand and pulled her down on top of him. She shifted so his erection was between her thighs, and then she bent and took him in her mouth.

He never said a word after that.

Time passed and they might have slept a little, but when he looked around for her she was missing. He sat up quickly, then saw her in the bathroom speaking to someone on the phone.

"Mom. It's snowing hard. I could try to get home, but it might be best if I wait until morning."

He could only hear the one sided conversation, but it was enough to make him pump a fist into the air. "Okay, if you're sure. Tell the girls I love them, and that I'll be back first thing in the morning. And since it's Christmas Eve, we can each open one present from under the tree." She laughed, and spoke quietly. "Yes, Mom. He is very nice. Now I've gotta go. Love you, Bye." He was sitting up in bed, with two pillows behind him when she returned. The covers came up to his belly button. He opened her side and invited her in.

She watched him for a minute. "You heard?"

"I did." A grin spread across his face. "I'm glad. It was a smart decision."

"Oh, yeah? Why is that?"

"Because I'm going to give you an early Christmas present later. After we open a fine bottle of wine. And caviar. You like caviar?" He sprang out of bed, and grabbed her hand. "Come on with me to the kitchen. We'll have a picnic. But first I heard the dogs whining. Better let them out, and then we can have a feast."

"Are you for real?"

He winked at her. "Feel me and see."

She laughed. "I can't figure out how you stayed single this long." Her eyes narrowed. "Unless you have a whole lot of ex-wives stuffed in an attic, or under the bed."

"Wow. You've got some imagination." He patted her backside. "Maybe I'm just particular. Waiting for that right woman to walk into my life."

"And has she?"

"I think so." He kissed the top of her head. "Time will tell."

Still naked, they entered the kitchen together. The dogs yipped and ran around in circles. Rasco had left a present for him next to the glass window. He cleaned it up, then opened the door and let them run threw. He shivered. "Damn. That's cold. You want a robe or a blanket? No point in getting dressed, because I'm just going to end up taking it off."

She lifted a brow and put a hand on her hip, making him want to take her right then and there. "Oh. Is that right?"

"You keep looking at me like that, you'll see."

"You'd have to catch me first." Laughing, she ran off into the living room and ducked behind a couch. Just as he got near, she ran off again. He grabbed a throw pillow and flung it at her, and she tossed it right back. He was on one side of the couch. She on another. Cat and mouse.

Only one way to catch the mouse he decided, and hurled himself over the back of the couch before she could slip away. He rolled her on top of him and they lay like that, laughing, breathing hard, and then they were kissing again. He found a blanket, and wrapped her in it.

"Stay warm," he said, and stood up. "Want to watch TV?" He put it on, and then went into the bedroom for his flannel robe. He tied it loosely around his waist, then sauntered back into the living room. Jennie had let the dogs back in, and they were sitting on the couch next to her.

"Gone two minutes," he muttered, "and you already replaced me."

She picked up a pillow, and patted the seat next to her. "I saved room for you."

"Later, baby." He opened the door to the pantry, found a can of dog food and put half in each bowl, adding some kibbles along with it.

The dogs went after the food, and the girl was all his.

"Ah. Now, I have you all to myself."

"Think you can handle me?"

"I'm sure going to try." He kissed her again, thinking that a man could get used to this. No wonder so many men got married—if they had a woman like this.

"What are you smiling about?" she asked softly.

"I finally figured it out."

"What?"

"Why so many men have wives."

She glanced at him, her eyes wary. "Seriously? That's what you were thinking?"

"Uh-huh. I think they're on to something." He slipped an arm around her and she dropped her head on his shoulder. "This is nice."

CHAPTER NINETEEN

Jennie's pulse leapt with pleasure and she melted a little more. Like the last winter snow before the rebirth of spring, the ice around her heart began to thaw. She was not a wide-eyed young woman falling in love for the first time. She knew love and loss, and hurt and betrayal. She had lived thirty-one years and knew that some men would say anything to get into a girl's skirt, but she honestly believed Nick and the beautiful words he spoke to her. He was genuine, the real deal.

"This is better than nice," she said softly. "You have given me a wonderful night to remember." And hope for the future, she didn't add.

After all, she'd be leaving for the winter and wouldn't be back this way again until she sold her home and the girl's were out of school. July or August, perhaps. Anything could happen in that amount of time. So whatever feelings they had for each other were not going to have a chance to grow. It was almost a relief as she wasn't ready to love again. One day she'd embrace it open heartedly. But she needed to mourn Daniel a little longer.

Their love, their marriage deserved that. He deserved that.

"I hope it's more than just one night. I want you to remember me. And everything we've done, and the way I feel about you."

She buried her head into Nick's shoulder, and snuggled against his warm body as they sat on the couch holding hands. Naked, vulnerable, she should have felt anything but safe. But that was how she felt. Nick made her feel safe. Protected. As if he wouldn't let anything bad happen to her.

"I will. I promise."

He kissed the top of her head. "Stretch out on the couch. Sleep a little. I'm going to put a few things together, open up some wine, find some music, and then wear you out again." His eyes were smiling. "You might want to rest up."

"I feel rested. Sated. But I would like to shower. How about if I freshen up for round two while you work the kitchen."

He chuckled. "That sounds good too."

She dropped the blanket and gave him a good rear end view as she headed for his bathroom. She ran the water hot and stepped underneath, soaping herself, eyes closed, head thrown back. She couldn't remember the last time she had felt so sensual, so alive, and happy. She felt happy. Her heart fluttered, and she put a hand on her chest. Dear heaven! It was a sobering thought. Did she have a right to be happy?

Yes, came the answer.

She opened her eyes and looked at the ceiling to see if there was a crack somewhere, a direct route to heaven. Surely that had been Daniel who had answered. The steam rose in the bathroom, and she smiled, feeling his presence, his acceptance and his love. He would not want her to be unhappy. Or alone. He would want a man like Nick in her life and in his children's.

The thought made her shiver. She was about to step out of the shower, when she felt a warm body step in. "You leaving so soon?" Nick whispered, cupping her bottom.

"Maybe not."

"Good. I figured I could use a shower too."

His mouth captured hers and kissed her deeply. Her knees grew weak and she had to hold on to his shoulders for support. She felt his erection beating against her tummy and guided him inside of her. She wrapped one leg around his back as he rammed her against the shower wall. It was fast. Furious. And super hot.

She bit his shoulder and cried out his name. He pumped harder, and with a bellow he came. Boneless, she slid to the floor of the shower stall, and he slid down next to her. The stream of the hot water poured down and they were too weak and washed out to turn the tap off. After several minutes, Nick regained enough strength in his legs to stand, turn off the water, and help her up. He toweled her dry, then gave her one of his flannel shirts to wear.

"You ready for that glass of wine now?"

She smiled. "Never readier." She laughed softly. "I think I've earned it."

"You have. I opened my finest. A very nice Chateauneuf du pant. I bought it at a wine auction last year. Kept it for a special occasion." His eyes held hers. "This is it."

Oh, my! He did know how to make a girl feel special! "Wow. I don't know what to say to that."

"You can say thanks, later. Right now, I want to know what you think of it."

She followed him to the kitchen, feeling special, and cared for. Dare she use the word—loved? "You didn't need to do this. I like wine, but I'm not a connoisseur, or anything."

"That's not important. But I did want to share it with you." He handed her the glass of wine and lifted his glass.

"What shall we drink to?" she asked.

"How about our chance meeting? And to continuing our friendship? I think that's worth a toast, don't you?"

"I certainly do." They clinked glasses, their eyes on each other as they took their first sip.

She watched him roll the liquid around his tongue, savoring the taste before he swallowed, and she did the same. It was a full-bodied wine, smooth, complex, and delicious.

"Tell me about it," she said. "What's the history, and how come you bought it at an auction?"

He showed her the label. 2012 Chateau de Beaucastel. "This particular wine comes from a famous family-owned estate in the Rhone Valley. They have a great reputation, treating the vineyard like a garden. No chemical fertilizers, only organic. They've won a bunch of awards." Nick shrugged. "I discovered it one summer while I was apprenticing in France." He rolled the wine around his glass before taking another sip. "This has a rich flavor of dark and blue fruits, a hint of licorice and something else I can't identify."

He laughed when she nearly choked on her wine. "Okay. I read up on the ingredients. But I did visit the vineyards. And the auction was last year. A charity event."

Lips tasting like the delicious wine, she gave him a quick kiss. "Thank you for sharing this. It's unbelievable. I'm a lucky girl to be here tonight."

"I'm the one who's lucky."

Oh, God—but she wanted to do him again. He was the most romantic man she'd ever met! "Stop! Please stop! I can't take anymore sweet talk, or I'll lose my head." And my heart, she didn't add. But it was definitely on the line. Too close for comfort.

"No more sweet talk. I promise." He moved away from her and took a few trays out of the fridge. The Russian black caviar he'd promised. Smoked salmon with onions and capers. "We can nibble on this, and then I'm going to fry up some crab cakes that I made earlier, and we can have that with a green salad. Quick and easy."

She rolled her eyes. "My idea of quick and easy is a frozen pizza."

He grimaced and shuddered in mock horror. "Say it isn't so."

"Okay. Maybe not a frozen pizza, but one ordered and delivered."

"I'll allow that, and I'm not above it either." He cracked a smile. "We really should be having shots of iced vodka with the caviar. "Want some?"

"Won't it ruin the taste of the wine?"

He took her glass. "We can have the wine with the crab cakes, but smoked salmon and caviar definitely requires vodka."

Jennie smiled and hitched her butt on a kitchen stool, happily content to let him lead in the kitchen. Shots of vodka, good wine and hot sex was a tasty but dangerous combination. But she wouldn't complain tonight. Come what may, tonight was hers, and she was taking it.

They entwined their arms and downed a couple of shots, laughing with the novelty. As they nibbled on the food and each other, each taste seemed like a rare gift. The caviar exploded on her tongue, the smoked salmon was moist and delicious as it slid down her throat. The rich wine lingered on her tongue and in their kisses long after it was gone. The joy was fleeting Jennie knew, but all the sweeter for it.

* * *

The sky was still dark when Nick woke and discovered he was alone. He'd reached out a foot to touch hers, and then a hand but came up empty. Startled, he rose from the bed, but then he stopped moving when he heard something. Weeping. Huge sobs that tore at him and made him ache too.

He had wondered when the tears would come. The senseless guilt. The unhappy thought that she was actually happy. It had been too much to hope that she would have gone unscathed from their afternoon and evening together. He'd never be the same man again.

He knocked gently on the bathroom door. "Jennie? Can I come in?"

There was no answer, only the sound of a huge gasp, a fit of coughing, followed by another heart wrenching sob. He tried the door handle and found it unlocked. He slipped inside but didn't turn on the light. His eyes adjusted and he saw her on the floor, sitting on the bathroom mat, her back against the shower door. He remembered taking her in the shower, but that memory was for another time. Right now, he needed damage control.

He knelt down, put his hands on her shoulders, and his forehead against hers. "Come back to bed and cry in my arms."

She put a hand to her mouth, made a horrible wailing sound, and then cried harder. He didn't know what to do. He tried to take her in his arms, but she flung them off. Leaving her was not an option, so he sat down on the bare tile ready to wait it out.

She made some keening noises, guttural sounds that were so deep and forlorn that they had to come from the soul. He hated doing this to her. He had only meant to make her happy, and for a little while he had.

He placed his hand on her bare leg, and just left it there. Eventually the sobbing lessoned, the wailing and keening noises died away, and she covered her face in shame. Between hiccups, she said, "Go away. Please. I don't want you to see me like this."

"Too late," he answered with a sheepish smile. "And I'm not leaving you until you forgive yourself." He stood up and ran the cold water, then put a wash cloth under it, rang it dry and handed it over. "Here. Wash your face. There's a hand towel and tissues on the sink. I'm going to get you a glass of water and an Advil. And then you and I are going to sit on the couch and have a long talk."

"Damn you." She sniffed, but used the cloth to dab at her ravaged face. "Please stop being so nice. You're killing me." Another sob ripped loose and he used that as an excuse to grab the water and pink pill.

He might take one himself.

In the kitchen, he did just that, then walked back into the bathroom with hers. She was standing at the sink now, shoulders bent, head down, splashing cold water on her swollen eyes and face. "I don't want you looking like this when you leave," he said gently. "I'm going to have you sit on the sofa with cold compresses. The girls will be upset if they see your eyes red and puffy from tears."

"They're used to it by now."

He swallowed a lump in his throat and stroked her back.

She flinched and he removed his hand. He knew pity was hard. He'd felt the sharp edge of it many times in his younger years from well-meaning people. He couldn't pity her, and he didn't. He only wanted to offer comfort and understanding.

"Not on my account," he answered. "And not on my watch."

He stepped back, giving her some space. "Take a shower. Get dressed or not. I'm going to make us some coffee and we are going to sit and talk this out. You have nothing to feel bad about. And I don't believe for one minute that it was a mistake. Or that our feelings aren't real."

With that he turned around and left, not sure if he'd already said too much. She needed to process things. Time and distance would give her better clarity.

CHAPTER TWENTY

Jennie and Nick drank their coffee and sat and talked it though, but it didn't change anything, or make Jennie feel better. She *knew* she had done nothing wrong and probably Daniel would have given her his blessing, but that didn't alleviate her guilt, or the deep-seated knowledge that she wanted to do it again.

Fact was—she didn't want to let Nick go. And yet, she had to. After the holiday she was leaving. Going back to Norfolk. Six months would pass and she couldn't expect him to wait for her. He cared about her, she knew that, but love was a different story. They weren't in love. They didn't know each other well enough for that. And they didn't have the luxury of time to explore their feelings deeper.

And so, after their coffee and their talk, Jennie picked up her new pup, Rasco, and put him in the small crate she'd left in the back of the rented SUV.

"You drive safely," Nick said, standing next to the open door of the car. "And have a wonderful Christmas. Give my best to the kids and your mom and dad." His jaw was set, his voice steady. "And I hope I see you when you come back for your car, but if I don't I'll understand."

His eyes searched hers, but she lowered her chin, unable to look him in the eye. Her stomach was churning, and every cell in her body ached. Yes, her body had done a major workout, but that was not what hurt. Leaving Nick standing here alone was almost unbearable. He deserved love, and a family, and all the happiness in the world, but he had to choose it, and so far he hadn't. He'd offered her a glimpse of what it would be like to have him as a permanent partner in her life, but that's all it was. A glimpse.

"How is it that you understand me so perfectly?" she said slowly, still unable to look at his beautiful face. "And yet, I don't understand you at all." She was hanging on by a thread, so afraid that she'd never see him again, and yet afraid that if she did, she'd lose what she had left of Daniel. She couldn't have both.

"What don't you understand?" He lifted her chin. "I think you know more about me than you realize. You might not trust it, that's all."

Her lips trembled, and he ran his thumb over her bottom lip. "I do trust you. I ache for you. You have so much to offer a woman and yet you don't."

"Jennie…"

"Don't. Don't say anything. I have to go. Let's just sit on this for awhile and see where it takes us." She jumped into the car and gazed down at him. "I'm sorry about everything. I care about you more than you know…"

"Jennie…" his hand reached for her but she left it hanging.

She blinked back tears. "Thank you for last night. It was one of the best nights of my life." She released a heart-felt sigh. "I wish you could be with us for Christmas, Nick. I will miss you very much. But the kids... I can't do this to them. The insecurity, the thought that they might have a replacement father. It's not right."

"I know that, Jennie. It's the best thing to do." He gave her one long last glance then stepped away from the car. His shoulders were straight, his posture erect as he walked back to his house. He turned at the doorstep and gave her a wave and a small, sad smile. She knew he was not as unaffected as he let on. Inside he hurt too.

Heart breaking, she put the car in gear, found the highway and headed out of town.

She was home by eight a.m. The kids were eating breakfast when she bounced in. Whatever she felt in her heart had to remain guarded, and not exposed to her family at this holiday time. She would be cheerful even if it killed her.

"Good morning children," she called, smiling brightly. "Morning Mom and Dad."

She kissed everyone, hoping that she didn't look as different as she felt. Her eyes were a little red rimmed, but due to the icepacks Nick had given her the puffiness was gone. "I have a surprise for you. An early Christmas Eve present," she said to her kids.

"What is it?" they both asked, jumping up and down on their seats. They pushed their plates with the remnants of egg on toast to the side. "Can we have it now or do we have to wait until tonight? We usually get a present after dinner," Katie said to her sister, knowing the routine well.

"Today is a very special day, and this little present won't wait." Jennie laughed. "Grab your jackets and come on out to the car. You can have your present now."

Nana and Papa knew about the dog so they gave her a nod and a smile, cleaning the plates away, and allowing the girls to leave the table without their breakfast eaten. It was the day before Christmas and they were getting a pup, a poor replacement for the dad they loved and lost, but would bring a smile to their sweet faces.

The girls followed her out the door, both of them trying to guess what the present would be. "I hope it's a cell phone," Katie said. "Then I can call all my friends from school. So cool."

"No, sweetheart, no cell phone. Not for a few more years."

"I think it's the i-Pad I asked for," Brooke said hopefully. "I already know how to use it, and some of my friends have their own tablets. Even if I am young, I wouldn't drop it or lose it."

"Not this year, Brookie, my love. You still can borrow mine."

They'd only be little girls for a short time.

"Okay, close your eyes." Jennie opened the back door of the SUV. "Now open them."

They opened their eyes wide and squealed with delight.

"It's the puppy," they cried. "Spotty," Brooke said.

"Mommy, can we hold him?" Katie asked, hands already reaching out for the small dog.

"*Arf, arf.*" Rasco ran around his cage in circles, his tail wagging joyfully. "*Arf. Arf.*"

"He's happy to see us," Katie cried. "Oh, this is the best present of all."

Jennie clipped a new collar and leash on the young pup before she opened the door. "Okay, we can let him out now, but hold on tight to the leash. You know how this guy loves to run."

She handed Rasco over to the two girls, who took turns hugging him and accepting his wet kisses. "Nick has been taking care of him and he named him Rasco, because he says the pup is a little rascal. I think it's cute and suits him but if you girls want to name him something else, that's fine. It's up to you, but it doesn't have to be decided immediately."

"Hey, Rasco," Brooke said, burying her nose in the dog's sleek coat of hair. "Do you want to be Spot or Rasco?"

"*Arf, arf,*" the dog answered, wagging his tail so hard his bottom half moved.

The girls laughed and put the squirming dog on the ground. "Take him around the side of the house and let him pee before coming inside," Jennie told them. "But hold on tight to the leash."

She watched the pup hopping in the snow. The girls' happy faces made her heart lift with pleasure. This is what the season was all about. Love and giving, and family. She was very blessed to have so much in her life to be thankful for.

And yet, even though she smiled as the dog and her kids ran around in the snow, she couldn't help but think of Nick and how alone he truly was. Right this minute he'd be in the kitchen of his bistro cooking up a special meal for his customers tonight. He said the place was sold out and he planned to make bouillabaisse, a flavorful seafood stew. He also had filet and lobster tails as a second choice.

He was successful in his own right, took pride in his work and bistro. And she knew that his love for cooking had been an extension of his love for his grandmother. She must have been a very special woman to have raised this child of her heart that her own daughter had discarded. It occurred to Jennie that perhaps it was his mother's rejection that had damaged him somehow—his fear of commitment, his preference to live life alone.

"Hey, Mom." Brooke stood in front of her, chin in the air as she glanced up at her mother's face. "Rasco made three yellow puddles, and Katie and I don't have our hats or mittens on." She shivered. "My ears are cold. My hands too. Can we come back inside?"

Jennie gasped. "Oh, man. I'm sorry! I got lost in the moment and didn't even think about your hats and gloves." She only wore a jacket as well, but her mind was occupied elsewhere and she hadn't noticed the cold. Guilt hit her full force. "Give me the leash and run inside. Get next to the fire."

The girls took off, leaving her with Rasco. No more thoughts of Nick.

* * *

Nick was dicing up the ingredients for his bouillabaisse when Ally walked in. "What are you doing here so early," he asked, turning the dutch oven on medium high. He

177

PATRICE WILTON

added olive oil, onion, fennel, and garlic into the pot to
sauté.

"Just popped in to see if you need any help." She
shrugged out of her jacket and removed her wool cap
from her blue-black hair. Her big brown eyes were
shining and looked full of mischief. "So how did last
night go?"

"It went." He answered in a noncommittal kind of
voice that discouraged more questions. "She had to leave
and get back to her kids."

"Hmm. That's too bad." Ally picked up the rubber
spatula and began to stir the onions. "Starting to brown.
Should I add the wine now?"

"Yeah. Turn it down." He pushed over a dish with the
zest from a couple of oranges, the large bowl of diced
tomatoes in juice, peeled and diced potatoes, then the
clam juice in her direction. "Add these and the saffron, if
you're going to stick around and bother me."

"Then do I bring it to a boil?"

"Yes. Thanks." He stuck his hands in his pockets,
leaned against the counter, and studied her. "So what are
you really doing here?"

"I wanted to see how you're doing. I felt kind of bad
declining your invitation to dinner without giving you a
proper excuse." She dropped the potatoes into the large
pot, being careful not to splatter. "My parents are coming
here to Philadelphia to see me. I can't go home."

He frowned, giving her a curious look. "Why can't you
go home? If you need more days, all you have to do is
ask."

"It's not that." She turned to face him. "I can never go home. It's not safe."

"What do you mean?" He walked over to Ally, and took her by the shoulders. "What's going on with you?" He studied her face. "Why do you work here when you have the talent to make a name for yourself?"

"I don't want to make a name for myself. That's the problem. I can't let anyone know where I am or how to find me." Her brown eyes darkened and she pulled away, straightening her shoulders. "I dated a guy in college. Six months. And when I tried to break it off he threatened to kill me. He stalked me, followed me from class to class, hung around my dorm. Scared the shit out of me." She rubbed her arms. "He broke my windshield, vandalized my room—I got a restraining order, but it did no good."

"Ally." That sucked. Nick couldn't even imagine scaring another person on purpose. Threatening their life. "The police can't do anything about this guy?"

"'Fraid not. So I quit school. Went back home, but he followed me there too. Everywhere I went he'd show up. Leaving obscene messages. The cops say they can't do anything because he never acted out his threats."

"That's bullshit."

"Guess I was supposed to wait until he killed me before the police could arrest him. I like living too much to give him the opportunity."

"I'm so sorry, Ally." He gave her a brief hug. "How long has it been?"

"Nearly two years." She blinked away tears. "I'm afraid to go home. My parents still see his car stalking the place.

They call the police, but before they get there he drives off. He's sick but not stupid."

"That really sucks." He was quiet for a few minutes. What could he do to help? "Are you safe living in that cabin down by the lake?"

"As safe as I'll ever be. I have it totally wired—the best security money can buy. And it's hooked up to the local police station, for however good they are."

"How about you? Do you have anything to defend yourself?"

"I'm trained in martial arts and I have a rifle next to the door." She ran a hand through her spiky hair. "I'm an excellent shot."

"Glad to hear it." He turned the pot down to medium and covered the bubbling stew. "If he ever comes near, you shoot that son-of-a-bitch."

"I intend to." She smiled in a hard way that made Nick view her completely different. "Anyway. If you don't have anything to do, you're welcome to go into the city with me and meet my parents. They are very curious about you." She tilted her head and folded her arms under her breasts. "So when did Jennie leave? Last night or this morning?"

"A couple of hours ago." He turned his back and started the Faux Rouille sauce to be added right before serving. He took out the sour cream, mayonnaise, minced garlic, paprika, and lemon juice and mixed them in a bowl. After it was perfectly blended, he covered it and stuck it in the fridge.

"Will you be seeing her again?"

The question hung in the air for a few long seconds, and Nick grunted out a reply. "Time will tell. She wants to buy a place near her family this summer. Meanwhile she'll be returning to Virginia. Her husband was killed in a helicopter crash. A training exercise." He swore. "It's tough on her and the kids. Not sure she's ready."

"I'll bet she is." Ally touched his arm. "And you. I've never seen you so gone on a girl before."

"She's pretty special, but I'm not sure if it's going anywhere. I still have things to do. Have to build this business and finish fixing up my grandparents' home to sell. Lots of details and financial decisions to take care of before I take on a responsibility of a wife."

"And kids," she added. "How do you feel about that?"

"That doesn't bother me. I kind of like the idea." He wasn't sure that he wanted children of his own. Passing on his genes might not be a great idea. But he kept that thought to himself.

He ran a hand over his jaw and grimaced. "I really like her, Ally."

"I know you do. Just want you to be happy, that's all, boss." She grabbed her jacket. "Let me know about tomorrow. You're still welcome to come with me. It'll be fun."

"I'll think about it and let you know first thing in the morning," he answered cautiously.

Ally jammed the knit hat onto her head, her brown hair barely visible "Okay. Got a few last minute gifts to buy. See you at noon."

"Thanks, Ally. For everything."

This conversation had been an eye-opener—given him a whole lot of insight into her behavior, and why she'd never wanted to sell her photos or make a living doing what she did best. He'd do anything in his power to protect her. In the past hour, they'd moved from employer and employee to being friends.

He liked that.

CHAPTER TWENTY-ONE

Jennie helped her mother prepare their Christmas Eve dinner, while the children played with the dog and attempted to keep him away from the tree. They ended up having to barricade it so the pup wouldn't sniff around and tear at the wrapping. An hour in the house, and already one present destroyed.

"So how did things go last night?" her mom asked quietly.

Jennie looked up from the platter of smoked salmon she was arranging on a plate. "It went incredibly well. It was this morning that was a problem. I had a total meltdown."

"Oh, Jennie. I thought your eyes looked a little bloodshot when you first showed up." She reached out and stroked her back. "I'm so sorry. It was only to be expected. How did Nick take it?"

"Like the perfect gentleman he is. He was patient, sweet, understanding. It just made things worse. If it had only been about sex it would have been easier on both of us. But we have feelings. How long they last will be anyone's guess."

"None of us can bet on a future, honey. You, most of all, know that. But he does care about you, and the girls. No one has tied him down yet."

"That's true, but we won't see him for half a year—if at all. I mean what are the chances that he'll not have a girlfriend by next summer? That would be ridiculous."

"When you return for your car, spend a night. Don't rush off. And keep in touch over the winter. Email, text, do what you have to do to keep your memory alive."

"I'm not sure that I can do that, Mom. Part of my crying jag was that while I like him a lot, I'm not ready to stop loving Daniel. It's too soon to let those feelings go. I can't love two men, Mom. It wouldn't be fair to either of them."

"Only one of them is here, in Heaven, Pennsylvania. Poor Daniel is in God's hands now."

Jennie bit her bottom lip and sucked back tears. She'd cried enough for a lifetime, and she was still worn out from last night's sex-binge. "I know. I understand that. Maybe this winter will give me some closure. If by spring Nick is still available and I feel ready to take that next step, well, then it was meant to be."

She sliced up some onion and added that and capers to the dish, then covered it with plastic wrap. "Salmon's done. What else can I do?"

"Well, we are having a beautiful pork tenderloin which is marinating in a nice wine sauce. I made scalloped potatoes, your dad's favorite, but we need to decide on broccoli or asparagus. Which do your girls like best?"

"Broccoli, but I'm not sure if they will eat it tonight. They love your potatoes and pork roast, and they still have tiny appetites."

They heard a loud snore coming from the family room, and Jennie smiled. "Dad looks tuckered out. How has be been doing lately?"

"Much better. He's been going to rehab three times a week, and is slowly rebuilding his strength. But the medicines make him tired, I think."

Jennie yawned. "I didn't get much sleep myself. Think you could handle the girls if I napped for an hour?"

"Of course. You run off. I'm glad he wore you out," she added with a twinkle in her eye.

"Mom!"

"Don't Mom me. Just be glad I'm hip enough to appreciate what a good man can do."

Jennie rolled her eyes and told her kids she was going to lie down for a short nap. "Have fun with Rasco, and try not to wake Papa. He needs his sleep. When I get up we can all go out for a walk around the block. See the lights I promised you."

"Okay, Mom. We're okay," Katie said. "We love Rasco. Best present ever!"

Jennie went upstairs to her room and climbed under the covers. With her eyes closed Nick's handsome face came to mind. The tenderness and concern in his deep brown eyes when he looked at her, the way his lips would twitch when he was amused, the full sexiness of his smile. He was the kindest, most considerate man she'd ever met—next to her husband. They were both equally good men, and to have met two in her lifetime and to be loved by both, made her a very lucky woman indeed.

She did feel loved by Nick, but whether it was a love that would survive and flourish was still unknown. She hoped it would, because she had a feeling that with the sale of her house, she'd be ready to move on in every aspect of her life.

Last night had been a giant leap forward. She tingled remembering the things he did to her, and she to him. He was a passionate, considerate lover, and had surprised her and pleased her in more ways than she could have imagined.

And she very much wanted to do it again. The thought of him making love with another woman made her heart hurt. She couldn't imagine him doing it with anyone but her, at least not anytime soon. She prayed that she was right.

An hour later, Jennie slipped out of bed, and took a shower. Refreshed, she returned downstairs to take her kids and new pup for a walk in the neighborhood. It was half past four, but the daylight had disappeared, and a great many of the homes were festively lit.

"Okay, kids. Let's go get some fresh air before dinner, and we can talk about our Christmas wishes."

Brooke clapped her hands. "I wished for a puppy and it already came true."

"I wished to make you girls happy, and I did," Jennie told them with a hug and kiss each. "What did you do when I was napping?" she asked. "You were so quiet, I didn't even hear you."

"We helped Nana wrap presents for Jed and Jake," Katie told her. "They got some new pajamas and Gap sweatshirts, and some board games. Kind of cool."

Jennie helped bundle up the children, tucking scarves around their necks, then she donned her own wool coat and hat. Once they were warmly attired she bent down to check that the dog's collar was secure before they all ventured outdoors.

Hand in hand they walked around the community—a pleasant blend of retired couples and younger families with children. It was easy to identify which was which as the seniors usually had lights around their windows and on their bushes or trees, others had candles in all the windows. The families with children were a little more obvious, with blown up Santa Clauses and reindeers on their lawns. The girls critiqued the snowmen the other children had made.

Rasco tugged at his leash, jumping excitedly around the girls' legs and getting himself tangled up. He left yellow snow everywhere he went, determined to mark his territory from one house to another. How one little dog could have so much pee was beyond her, but Rasco seemed quite proud of it.

After a half hour they returned home. Nana gave the girls hot cocoa, while she poured eggnogs for the adults. The scent of the log fire and the pork roast in the oven drifted throughout the warm house. This is what she'd come home for.

Papa, awake, waved the girls over to him. "Come my little beauties, and tell me what you saw." His face glowed from the fire, and he looked quite sprightly all of a sudden. "Did you spot any reindeers in the sky? Anyone shouting, "ho, ho, ho?""

The girls giggled and took a seat next to him. He put an affectionate arm around them and kissed the tops of their heads. "What time does Santa get here?" he asked. "I might sit up and have cookies with him."

Brooke shook her head. "You can't, Papa. He won't allow it. Santa only comes when everybody is asleep. I think he's shy."

Katie leaned over Papa's belly, and glanced at her younger sister. "Don't be a ninny. He's not shy. He just doesn't want anyone to see him. He's probably not even a real human being. More like an angel I think."

"He's not an angel," Brooke said firmly. "Is he, Papa? He's a person, a really good person who works very hard all year making presents for all the kids in the world. Especially the poor ones. He gives them extra ones because they deserve it."

"No, he doesn't," Katie said. "He treats everyone just the same. Except the bad ones. They don't get presents. Only a bag of coal. What's coal, Papa?"

"Yeah, what is it?"

"Well, I'll tell you a story about coal," Papa said, "but first we all need to take a taste of our drinks and make a Christmas toast."

He raised his glass of eggnog, and looked at his wife and Jennie. "Merry Christmas, Louise, the love of my life. And Jennie, my darling girl, we are so very happy that you're here with us and will be moving close by." Lastly, he clinked his glass with the girls' two mugs and said,

"And may Santa bring you everything your heart's desire."

Then they all took a sip from their drinks.

The taste of the eggnog brought back so many memories. It was a tradition to always have an eggnog, virgin or laced with rum or brandy as they decorated the Christmas tree. Again on Christmas Eve, before they each opened a present, and then on Christmas morning as they cleaned up after the gifts.

She was reminded of the nights with Daniel when the children would be in bed, and how they'd light a fire and sip eggnog as they waited for the girls to fall asleep so they could bring out the presents. Every memory was a happy one, and one she'd cherish.

Life changed, but remained the same. Her parents had started the traditions that she continued with her own family, and Katie and Brooke would carry them down to their children too.

She raised the glass again. "This is to Daniel, husband and father. May he have the most wonderful Christmas ever. We love you honey, and you're in our thoughts and our hearts this day and every day. Merry Christmas, my love."

They all drank to Daniel, and then Nana had an idea. "Let's all say one thing about your dad," she said to the girls. "The first thing that pops into our minds. I'll start." She cleared her throat. "I love the way your dad used to whistle while he worked. He'd be putting your toys together or doing something and would whistle a happy tune."

"And I loved how he knew how to work all these fancy gadgets, like i-Pads and hooking us up with Netflicks." Papa smiled. "That man could do anything."

"And I loved jumping on him, and his pancakes on Sunday morning," Brooke said.

"I loved it when I was little and he used to put me on his shoulders so I could watch the parade. And his laugh. And his hugs. Everything," Katie said with tears in her eyes.

Jennie nodded. "And I loved how much he loved you all—his precious daughters that he loved more than anything, and his love for me, and for you Nana, and you Papa. He was the best husband and father that anyone could hope for." Tears blurred her eyes, but she raised them up, and whispered. "Thank you for the joy and love you gave us. We will miss you always."

Then she turned to her family. "Okay. Drink up, and then we should find one present to open." She wiped her eyes and smiled. "After all it's the night before Christmas."

"And all through the house, not a creature was stirring, not even a mouse," Katie said, and snuggled up to her Papa. "Do we have any mice in here?"

"We better not," Papa said, hugging both children. "And if we do, Rasco will scare them away. Won't you, Rasco?"

Hearing his name, he *arfed*, and made a running jump, landing on the sofa next to Brooke. He buried his head in her lap, looking for some loving too.

"Ah, Rasco. We forgot about you. Does he have a present, Mommy? He needs a present too."

"He's got some new toys," she answered with a smile. "He will have a fine Christmas, just like the rest of you."

CHAPTER TWENTY-TWO

Jennie woke up Christmas morning, thinking of Nick. Alone. Her heart ached for him. It didn't seem like he had any close friends or family to spend the holiday with and the thought of him spending the day by himself was just so sad. What had happened in his life, she wondered, to have arrived at this place with no one to love or who loved him?

It wasn't right, not for such a kind, good-hearted man. And yet, she knew it was his doing. He had told her that he had lady friends, so obviously he chose bachelorhood, it wasn't forced upon him.

Still, knowing his loneliness was self-imposed didn't alleviate her concern over him, or diminish the longing she had to hold him tight and never let him be lonely again. Her eyes burned with unshed tears. He would hate it if he knew she felt sorry for him, because he was not a man to be pitied. He was bright, charming, handsome and successful, and had everything outwardly that a man could want. And yet, inside he was still that lost child without a mom, or parents of his own.

She glanced at the bedside clock. It was six a.m. and the house was quiet. Hopefully, she still had a few minutes before the girls woke up, and the ensuing chaos of opening presents began. Her sister's family would be arriving after lunch, so the excitement and noise on this Christmas morning would be partially contained. At least to a dull roar.

She thought she heard a giggle coming from the room next door but decided to ignore it as long as she could. When the girls were ready they'd pounce on her and drag her downstairs to see what Santa bought.

Meanwhile she could snuggle here in peace. Precious peace where she could think of Daniel, celebrate a moment alone with him, and accept the things she couldn't change. She sent a little prayer heavenward and told Daniel how much she still loved him and always would. She asked him to forgive her for the growing feelings she had inside of her for another man. Knowing Daniel he would want her to be happy, but they'd always been honest with each other and this was no time to stop.

Jennie heard the door creak open, and there were the girls. Katie and Brooke peeking in on her. She tossed the covers back and opened her arms wide. "Come here you little munchkins."

With a whoop of glee, they ran to her, jumped on the bed and were enfolded in her arms.

"Santa came," Katie cried out. "I looked over the railing and there's presents everywhere. He came. I can't believe he found us."

Brooke sat up and said very seriously, "I can. I told him when we were at the mall. And he promised he wouldn't forget." She giggled. "I'm so excited. Merry Christmas, Mom. Merry Christmas, Katie. And Merry Christmas, Daddy in heaven."

Jennie kissed her daughter's cheeks, then slipped out of bed. "Let me get my robe and brush my hair and teeth, then we'll go down to see what's in your stockings. Nana and Papa should be up soon."

The girls waited patiently for her on the bed, then as soon as she left the bathroom, they grabbed her hand and dragged her down the hallway to the staircase. She could smell the scent of hickory coffee in the air. Someone was up—unless it was Santa Claus!

"Good morning sleepyheads," Nana called out. "I expected the little ones to be down here bright and early."

Katie and Brooke ran to give their grandmother a hug. "Morning, Nana. Merry Christmas," the girls said.

Rasco danced around their feet, yipping and peeing in his excitement to see the girls.

"It is bright and early," Jennie said with a smile and hug for her mom. "Coffee smells good." She grabbed some paper towels and wiped up the mess on the floor.

"Help yourself to a cup. Papa is just taking a quick shower and will be here in a few minutes. The girls can do their stockings while they wait. Looks like Santa was very generous this year."

The girls squealed in excitement. "I love Christmas day, and Santa is the best!" Katie announced. "He works so hard all year through to bring presents to children all over the world. Do you think he gets paid to do that?"

Nana and Jennie exchanged amused glances. "I'm sure he does it through the kindness of his heart," Jennie said wisely. "And maybe charitable donations help him out financially to make all these special gifts."

"He's the best," Brooke said solemnly. "I love Santa Claus and his elves. They help too, don't forget."

"That's true. They have a big responsibility. They also feed the reindeer and navigate the flight around the world."

The little girls raised eyes big as saucers. "Holy cow. That's an important job. I'd like to feed the reindeer when I grow up," Brooke added.

Papa walked in, rubbing his belly. "Ho, ho, ho. Merry Christmas, everyone!"

The girls ran to hug him. "We love you, Papa. Merry Christmas everybody! Now we can open our stockings and our presents too!"

And for the next hour, that's what they did.

When all the gifts were opened and appreciated—with squeals of pleasure and a lot of hugs going around—Papa took a break to let Rasco out the side door. When the two of them returned, Papa and Jennie collected all the wrapping paper on the floor that Rasco was attempting to eat and toss around with decided glee.

"Where's his present?" Brooke asked her mother. "Doesn't he have a toy too?"

"Why, he certainly does. Try to keep him away from the tree and I'll go get it. It's still out in the car."

She came back a few minutes later with a Wal-Mart bag full of doggie chews, squeaky toys and puppy treats. "Here you go, girls. You can dole out the doggie gifts."

Figuring things were under control for the time being, Jennie escaped to shower and dress. Then she entered the kitchen to help her mother make eggs Benedict for the family breakfast.

"The girls loved their presents," Jennie told her mother. "You really knocked yourself out with all the gifts. And spoiled me too. Perfume, a gift card for Victoria Secret, and a day at the spa! Wow—I have never been so spoiled."

"We wanted to do something extra special for you and the girls this year, honey. We know how hard it's been on your own. We miss and love Daniel too." Her mother sniffed, and there were tears in her eyes when she said, "We just want you to find happiness again someday. Don't wait too long. Life can pass by so fast."

"I know, Mom. You're right. And I woke up thinking about Nick this morning, and his being all alone. If it's not too late, I'd like to give him a call and invite him for dinner. Would you mind?"

"Mind? We'd be delighted, and your sister is anxious to meet him. He will be very welcome." She smiled and her eyes were bright. "Go! Give him a call right this minute, before he gets another invitation."

She laughed. "I'll do that. Mind the English muffins. They're in the toaster."

"I can handle this. Off you go."

Jennie went into her bedroom to make the call. Nick answered after just one ring.

"Merry Christmas," he answered brightly, as though he'd forgotten that he didn't particularly like this holiday.

"Merry Christmas, Nick," she answered back. "What are you doing this morning? It's such a beautiful day."

"I'm at the farmhouse. Just doing a little interior work. There is still lots to be done and I figured with the restaurant closed, I might as well get started."

"Good heavens! Isn't it a sin to work on Christmas? No, I guess not. I forgot. I used to fly on Christmas day before I got married. Someone had to, and I thought, why not me?"

"Did you enjoy being a flight attendant? It's hard work, putting up with a lot of disgruntled passengers," he said.

"I did enjoy it. Mostly," she laughed. "I only flew for five years, but it gave me a chance to see places I never would have in my lifetime."

"That's the good part, I imagine."

"Anyway, enough about me. Tell me what you're doing at the house. I still haven't seen it, and want to before I leave. It just might be the perfect place for the girls and me. If you still intend to sell it, of course."

"I'm working on the upstairs bathroom. Put it a new commode and now I'm ripping up the old tile." He cleared his throat. "I'd be happy to show it to you when you return for your car. It's a good home—filled with happy memories and a lot of love."

"That's wonderful to hear. Thanks, Nick." She hesitated for a sec, wondering if this really was a good idea. It wasn't concern over what everyone's expectations might be, but the fact it would make leaving him more difficult. She couldn't seem to get him out of her thoughts. Just the idea of seeing him soon had her stomach doing butterfly hops. And she wanted a lot more of his kisses and good loving.

"How did the girls enjoy their morning?" he asked. "Were they excited about Rasco?"

"Oh yes! Of course. He was a big hit. Sweet dog. Nobody ever tried to claim him?"

"No. That's odd, right?"

"It is. But sometimes I think the whole accident was orchestrated from up above. Us landing in Heaven. Think about it—my airbag didn't even deploy."

"Well, I'm not sure about that being a part of the grand scheme of things, but I am glad to have met you, no matter the circumstance."

She left that hanging for a second, and then went for the gusto. "Me too, Nick. I really want to see you again. Can you come for dinner? Mom and Dad, the kids, Rasco, we all want you with us!"

"Are you sure?" he said cautiously. "You don't want to give anyone the wrong idea."

Did that mean he wasn't interested? Or that he was as unsure about their future as she was? Whatever it meant, she wanted to freshen his memory of what they had going on in the here and now.

"I am very sure. If you don't have other plans."

"Well, I guess the tile can wait another day." He chuckled. "Can't finish it off until spring anyway."

"Good." She grinned. "That's wonderful in fact." Her heart skipped with joy. "Around three thirty, four?"

"Give me the address and I'll be there."

She told him, and couldn't help but ask, "What would you have done if I didn't call?"

"I was planning on calling you with the excuse to ask about the dog. I've missed you, Jennie. A lot."

"Feeling's mutual." She gave a merry laugh. "You have made my day very special, Nick. Thank you for agreeing to come at the last minute like this. It's very sweet of you."

"It's my pleasure. I'll see you soon."

CHAPTER TWENTY-THREE

Nick completed the job at hand, ripping the remaining tiles off the bathroom floor. He placed them all in a heavy duty plastic bag to be toted downstairs and put in the bin. Funny thing was, the job didn't seem to be such a chore anymore, and he turned the portable radio up louder and sang along with some of the silly Christmas tunes.

What was getting into him? Puppies, children, enjoying Rudolph, the red-nosed reindeer, and getting excited about seeing the girls again. He would need to stop somewhere and find them a gift. Couldn't show up empty handed. But what was open, and what did you buy for little girls?

He knew the dog was enough to make the children happy, and bringing wine and chocolate would suffice, but he wanted to go the extra mile. This was going to be a hellova Christmas after all—the best present ever—a family gathering, a warm welcome into their home, to share in their joy.

His eyes grew misty thinking about it, and he wiped them with the back of his sleeve. Feeling foolish, he laughed at himself. He would hardly call himself a sentimental fool, but something about the holidays always made him melancholy.

His heart felt lighter than it had since he woke up yesterday morning to the sounds of Jennie crying. He hadn't thought he was at all ready for a woman in his life, and children? Not a chance.

Now the idea of seeing them, sharing a Christmas meal, watching the love and happiness in all their faces, made him realize that he didn't want to be alone anymore. He wanted a real family of his own. He wanted Jennie, and her sweet girls.

Guess that would mean he'd also get Rasco back.

He chuckled. He'd find a special gift for the mutt.

He was locking up, getting ready to leave when a light flickered in his brain. The attic! It was full of his grandparent's old belongings—some treasures there too. Didn't his grandma have an antique collection of porcelain dolls?

He ran up the stairs, grabbed a flashlight, then climbed the old rickety ladder to the attic. Switching on the dim light, he saw twenty or so old trunks and he'd have to go through them one at a time. His shoulders slumped, but he tackled the first one. It took him half a dozen attempts to find the collection of dolls—all lovingly wrapped in bubble wrap to preserve them for more decades to come. He counted eight in all, but for now he selected two. The pink one for Brooke, who declared it was her favorite color, the doll with the royal blue dress for Katie.

Going back downstairs with his treasures, he had a bounce in his step and a grin on his face. He knew how to win the girls' hearts, now all he'd have to do is figure out a way to win their mother's.

Nick locked up the house and drove back home, thinking about this unexpected change of plans. Luckily, he'd called Ally and declined her kind invitation to meet her parents in Philly. It would have been awkward at best. They might have believed that he had feelings for their daughter, when all he cared about was her well-being and keeping her safe. Jennie was the only woman he wanted in his life for keeps, and if she wasn't ready, well he was a patient man.

Once home, he let Sammy out, then left some food and water for his dinner. Because it was Christmas he put out a new dog toy and a large beef bone from the bistro for him to gnaw on.

Nick showered, shaved and got ready in a daze, slapping on some aftershave. What to wear? He dressed in navy slacks, a light blue checkered shirt with a tie, unsure if he should layer it with a cashmere sweater. He wanted to impress.

He cleaned the dolls up, careful not to mess up their fat curls. A convenience store might have Christmas bags, but he had white tissue just in case. He dusted off a very nice bottle of red wine, and took the box of Godiva that Ally had given him. It was already three, and for Christmas shopping, his options were limited.

Nick found the things he needed at the store, including a rawhide bone for Rasco, and a bouquet of flowers for the mom, then he was on his way to Jennie.

He found the address without any trouble. A big Lincoln SUV parked behind Jennie's Honda Pilot in the driveway, so he guessed that her sister and family were already here. He opened up the two bags he bought, put in the porcelain dolls, gathered the flowers, wine and chocolate, and made his way to the door.

He didn't have a hand to knock, but before he could rid himself of a parcel the door flew open and Jennie stood there. She was wearing black slacks and a glittery red jacket, and dangling Christmas earrings. Her cheeks were flushed pink, and her eyes sparkled. His pulse kicked up a notch and he thought she was the most beautiful woman in the world, and he, the luckiest man.

"Nick! You made it! I've been counting the minutes for the past hour." Her smile was wide. "What in the world did you bring?" She leaned in and gave him a warm kiss. "You look wonderful. Maybe we can ditch this party and sneak off alone?"

"Nick! Merry Christmas," John said from behind her. "Do come in. We're pleased that you could make it." He took the wine and chocolates out of Nick's hand. "You have excellent taste, I see."

"Thank you, sir. Thank you for having me." John had a hand behind Nick's back leading him toward the living room, where he could hear children laughing, and the adults engaged in lively conversation.

The girls squealed with delight when they saw him and ran into his arms. Rasco jumped on his legs, begging for attention. Jennie's mother rose from her chair and gave his cheek a kiss. "Thanks for coming on such short notice." Jennie, glued to his side, looked at her family. "Christy, Matt this is Nick."

They both left their seats on the sofa to shake his hand. "And these are our boys. Jed, the oldest, and Jake, our curious youngster." Christy laughed. "He wants to know if you have any more dogs like Rasco. He's in love with that puppy."

"Do you?" The boy asked with hope in his eyes. "Aunt Jennie said the dog just came from nowhere. Like a miracle."

Nick glanced at Jennie's pink cheeks, and then her family surrounding him, making him feel right at home. "No more pups, I'm afraid. All out of miracles."

He bent down and scratched the dog behind the ears then hugged Katie and Brooke. "I found something for you girls today. At my grandma's house. They used to belong to her." He handed them each a bag, hoping they'd like them.

"Antiques?" Jennie asked. "Be careful, you two."

"My grandma had them for a very long time." She'd loved kids and he knew that she'd approve of his passing them down.

Katie pulled out the beautiful porcelain doll with long auburn hair just like hers. The doll was dressed in a formal long royal blue dress with white lace at the collar and sleeves. "She's beautiful." Happy eyes looked up at Nick. "Can I play with her?"

"Of course you can. She's yours now."

Brooke pulled out her doll. "Thank you, Nick." She hugged the doll, then looked at her closely. "I like her, but her face looks kind of funny. Almost scary." She gave a little shiver. "Will she break?"

"Hopefully not," he told her, and inspected the doll's ivory face. "I know they're different than your usual dolls. These are special. Hand-crafted, so each one is different. Unique—like you and Katie. Not made in an assembly line like a Barbie doll." He winked at Jennie. "Although I'm kind of partial to Barbie myself. Always wanted to be Ken."

Everyone laughed, and Jennie stepped in, squeezing Nick's hand. "That was so thoughtful of you. You didn't need to come bearing gifts. Your being here is enough."

"I was thrilled you called. Heck, I had a busy day planned—laying down new bathroom tiles to be exact." He added for the benefit of Jennie's parents and sister's family, "I'm renovating my grandparent's old farm house."

"Well, you shouldn't be working on Christmas Day," Louise told him. "Glad you're here. We're all having a drink. What can John get you?"

"A glass of red would be great, thanks." He sniffed the air. "Something smells unbelievably good coming from the oven. You need any help in there?"

"Not today," Jennie told him leading him to a loveseat. "You're going to sit right down and be a guest, not a host." She linked her arm with his, and sat down close. "He works six days a week at the Bistro. Only has Sundays off," she told Christy and Matt.

They drank their pre-dinner drinks and had too many snacks—baked Brie, smoked salmon, and a heaping dish of giant shrimp with cocktail sauce.

The kids were playing with all their new toys, and Rasco had lodged himself on Nick's foot. He felt the length of Jennie's thigh pressed against his own. The family was warm and friendly, asking questions about his business and his personal life, but in a nice way. They obviously wanted to get to know him better, and if they were on the same page as him, he was all for that.

Sitting here with Jennie and her family brought to mind his years growing up with only his grandparents for company. He had been loved, there was no doubt about that, but it was vastly different than having siblings around and a doting mother and father too. Seeing the enormous ten foot pine tree, adorned so festively with gold and silver ornaments, twinkling lights, and all the opened gifts sitting on display under the tree, he could almost see why people liked Christmas. It was a day of giving, of expressing their love for each other. A day to communicate and celebrate not only their faith, but to bring back hope in the world for peace and love and understanding.

It might be a fantasy, but for the holiday season, that good will reached far and wide. Today Nick was glad to be a part of it.

CHAPTER TWENTY-FOUR

Before sitting down for their Christmas dinner, Jennie whispered in Nick's ear. "Let's take Rasco out for a quick walk." Her daughters were so engrossed with their new dolls that they didn't notice them slip out the door.

They had the pup on a tight leash as they walked to the edge of the property, next to the road. Once there, Nick let the leash run out, allowing the pup more freedom, but kept a firm grip so that Rasco couldn't run off. This was a dog that loved the thrill of the chase.

While the dog sniffed and marked his territory, Jennie took matters in her own hands. She wrapped her arms around Nick's waist and stood on tiptoe to give him a warm kiss. "I've wanted to do this since you walked in the door," she told him.

His mouth captured hers and his tongue slid inside. He kissed her with all the hunger in his soul and Jennie responded with the same degree of heat. Oh, how she wanted his kisses. She trembled with need and felt a yearning so deep inside that it was almost too much to bear.

"You're not the only one, sweetheart. Would anyone notice if we didn't come back?" His eyes danced with mischief.

"I think they might," Jennie laughed. "Probably send a posse out looking for us."

"In that case, I might need one more kiss to get me through the night."

She kissed him lightly, then wrapped her arms around his neck and looked into his face, wanting to memorize every detail. "I'm going to miss you so much when we go away."

"I will miss you more." He kissed her again, but then Rasco was back jumping on their legs, biting the leash, wanting to run, to play, to jump.

Sighing, Jennie said, "Guess this little guy needs a quick dash down the street. Come on. Let's race." She ran off and the pup and Nick overtook her.

At the end of the block, she leaned over, puffing out cold, harsh breaths. "Seems like I'm out of shape," she gasped.

"Trust me, babe, there is nothing wrong with your shape." He grinned at her, and her heart squeezed with love for this man.

How could she love him? They'd known each other less than a week. It was not possible, and she had to remember that. She was vulnerable. He was the first man she'd met since her husband died. He was handsome, charming, adorable, but until she left and returned to her regular life, she wouldn't know if this was real or just a holiday romance.

And yet, he was here, smiling at her with love in his eyes, and she wanted to believe in fairytales, new beginnings and happily-ever-afters. Why not? It was Christmas and she could believe in the magic for just a little while.

"Give me one more kiss, then we better get back inside."

"Bossy woman," he grumbled, putting an arm around her back, squeezing a knee in between her thighs, and letting her feel his need. "I might have to stay out here a few more minutes." He kissed her softly, then gazed into her eyes. "You have a wonderful family, and I can't thank you enough for letting me be a part of it. This is the nicest Christmas I've ever had."

Her heart hurt. She looked into his eyes, seeing all the pain and suffering that must have been there as a child. She wanted to spend the next fifty years making up for all that he'd lost.

She smiled gently. "I look forward to getting to know you better. *When* I return this summer, and *if* you haven't replaced me by then."

"How can anyone replace a woman like you?"

Her pulse quickened and she wanted to stay with him, but knew she had to go in. "I'll tell them you're taking Rasco around the block. Don't be long."

"I won't." He laughed. "Nothing that a little snow won't fix."

She stomped into the mud room and removed her coat and boots, then ran upstairs to wash up and apply more lipstick. He had clean kissed it off. She hugged herself tightly and grinned in the mirror. Who knew that while visiting her parents she'd take a side trip to Heaven?

When she returned downstairs, the 25 pound turkey sat resting on the counter. Potatoes and casseroles were coming out of the oven, and being transferred to the serving dish. Nick was already washed up and in the kitchen, offering his help. She smiled with pleasure, watching him mingle with her family and converse as if they were lifelong friends.

John glanced at Nick. "Would you do the honor and carve?"

Nick grinned, and picked up the tongs and carving knife. "It'll be my pleasure." Then with his normal expertise he laid layers of perfectly sliced white breast meat on one side of the platter and dark meat on the other.

He placed his masterpiece in the center of the table. "The turkey is perfect," he told Louise, making her blush with pleasure. "The meat is moist and just slightly pink in the middle. Couldn't have done a better job myself."

"Heavy words of praise, coming from a master chef like you." She grinned at him and bumped his shoulder. "Did you enjoy your walk outdoors? Wasn't too cold, was it?" She picked up a napkin and dabbed at his cheek, coming away with a lipstick stain. "Oops. You missed a spot." She laid a hand on his arm and lowered her voice. "You have made Jennie happy this Christmas. Thank you for that."

"Mom. Don't embarrass him." Jennie glanced at Nick's face, but he was staring at her with an expression that clearly stated he didn't mind. She felt her knees grow weak.

"Your daughter makes me happy too." He said it loud enough to be heard by everyone in the kitchen, and her heart swelled with pride.

Christy sent her a glance, and patted her beating heart, wiping moisture from her eyes. She went to the doorway to call the children in for dinner, whispering, "That man is definitely a keeper."

Jennie nodded. "I agree. If only…"

"Forget if only's. Don't let this slip away." Christy left her standing there to take her seat at the table between her two sons. Matt was at one end, and her father sat at the head. Louise chose the chair closest to the kitchen. Katie and Brooke sat between their Nana and Jennie, with Nick next to her.

John stood up and said grace. They all raised a glass in a holiday toast and sipped from their drink of choice. The children were fed first, and then the adults took turns, handing around the plates. Nick held the heavy platter of turkey in his hands, offering it to each of them, then settling the plate back down, he helped himself to his own.

Conversation flowed as easily as the wine. Matt turned to Nick and asked if was a football fan.

Nick swallowed and nodded. "That's why I close the restaurant on Sundays. To watch the games," he said with a grin. "I'm a Philadelphia Eagles fan. How about you?"

"I knew I liked you. Maybe you and I should go see a game sometime," Matt said, giving Christy a wink. "My wife hates football, and sitting in the stands in the dead of winter, but she doesn't mind my going."

"Sure. Call me. I can arrange for the tickets." Nick nudged his foot against Jennie's, letting her know that he was thinking about her, even if the men were monopolizing his conversation.

"What about baseball?" Matt asked. "Or fly fishing. Ever tried that?"

Nick grinned. "Sure have. Played baseball in my school days, and there's nothing better than catching striped bass in the Delaware River, and drinking a can of beer or two."

"Don't forget all the creeks around here stocked with trout." Matt laughed. "Sunday mornings in the summer I get up early and by the time the kids get out of bed, I'm back home with a cooler full of trout."

Not to be outdone, her father talked golf with Nick, who admitted he didn't have time to play, but enjoyed watching the games on a lazy Sunday.

He fit in, so quickly seeming to feel at home—almost magically he'd become a vital part of her loving family. Like a couple of teenagers, they played footsies under the table, and exchanged several warm glances, and it was one of the nicest Christmas's she could remember.

She wanted so much to believe that this was the fresh start she needed, and that he would become a permanent fixture in her life. Yet she was a realist and knew that after knowing Nick for less than a week, it was much too early to make that call.

Still, miracles do sometimes happen.

CHAPTER TWENTY-FIVE

The women cleaned up after dinner, while the men retired to the living room to hear Christmas music on Pandora and monitor the children's play. Her mother and sister could not say enough good things about Nick, and she had to whole-heartedly agree. Still, her feelings were raw, and as much as she adored Nick, a part of her longed for her husband, too. It was so cruel that Daniel was not with them tonight, that his life had been cut short. He'd never see his children grow into adults, or get ready for their first prom, or have the privilege to walk them down the aisle.

Life was unfair, and yet perhaps through a twist of fate it was offering her and her kids a second chance at happiness. As she thought this, Nick popped his head in, and heard his name being tossed about.

"My ears are burning," he said with a grin. "Thumbs up or thumbs down?"

"Up. Definitely up," Louise answered, and beckoned him over. "We have so many leftovers. Can I make up a care package for you?"

"No, that won't be necessary. I bring leftovers home from work."

"Oh, come. Just a few slices of turkey, a little stuffing, and we still have half that green bean casserole. Please take some."

"I will, if you insist. Dinner for tomorrow night. Might as well throw in a piece of that pecan pie so it won't go bad," he added, wrapping his arms around Jennie. His back was to the counter, and she fit nicely against him.

"I would invite you for tomorrow," she said, turning her head. "But we have tickets to Disney on Ice. The girls are going to love it."

"No problem. I still have a few things to catch up with before we reopen on Friday."

She sighed, and snuggled against the hard contours of his body. "I guess I won't get a chance to see you until it's time for us to leave. We have a lot going on for the next few days."

"I know. I wish it were different." He kissed the top of her head, and her mother pretended not to see. She wrapped up his pie and dinner and put it in a to-go container.

Jennie slipped out of his arms. "But you're going to show us your place before we leave. Maybe the girls can see the park with the carousel and Ferris wheel too."

"That's an excellent idea." He looked at the heap of pots and pans on the stove. "You want some help with that?" he asked her mother.

"Not a chance," Louise said, pushing him and her daughter out of the room. "You two go and relax. Spend some time together."

They sat on the sofa, but with all the children around, the background noise of the movie and the men chatting, it wasn't the romantic ending for the night she would have preferred.

Nick stuck around for another hour, then thanked everyone profusely for a wonderful night, and headed for the door. She slipped her coat on and walked him to his car.

She moved into his arms, and they kissed again—softly, gently, without the earlier heat and passion. They both knew it might be awhile before they could kiss like this again. A touch of sadness prevailed in the cool night air, taking away some of the Christmas magic that had made the day so bright.

Neither of them spoke about their worries, but both knew that a long winter was ahead, and promises would be foolish.

"Goodnight," she whispered, touching his cheek with the back of her hand. "Drive safely. I'll see you in a few days."

"Thanks for everything. It was the nicest Christmas I've ever had."

Tears sprang to her eyes. "You should have many more. You deserve the best, Nick. Don't settle for less."

"I won't. You and the kids have opened my eyes to what I've been missing. Although I do have a lot on my plate, I need to make room for people in my life. I want what you have—the love and joy of my own family, not just Sammy for company." He grinned. "Never thought I was ready to share my life with anyone, but I feel like I'm getting mighty close."

"Let me know when you do," she said softly, and then stepped away. She wouldn't push him. He had already given her so much, and even if he would perfectly fit into her life, she might not for his. After all, she was the mother of two young girls. He might want to find someone younger and have children of his own.

Jennie watched him get in the car and drive away, then returned inside. She took the girls upstairs to change into their pajamas, and she got out of her dressy Christmas clothes too. She put on a warm, fuzzy robe, and the three of them returned downstairs.

They turned on "It's a Wonderful Life", and even the children quieted down to watch the old classic. The kids drank cocoa while the adults had another drink of their choosing, and after a little while she heard her father's snores, and her girls nodding off. She took them upstairs to bed, and when she returned her sister's family was saying their goodbyes.

Jennie hugged her sister tight, overcome with emotion all of a sudden. It had been a lovely day, the first almost perfect day she'd had in the past year. Her heart yearned for so much, and was so full, yet so wanting, that she knew a meltdown was near.

"I'll see you tomorrow," she said to Christy. "I'm so glad you got tickets to Disney too. The girls love their cousins, even if they are boys. We can grab a bite to eat either before or after."

"The show is at four—why don't we plan on a late lunch, that way we can get home by seven. I don't like to be out late with all the crazy drivers," Christy said, making a face.

"Perfect. Pick us up around one thirty, and that will give us plenty of time to get something near the arena."

"You got it." Christy looked into her eyes. "Just want to say that Nick is wonderful. The real deal, and I think he is really into you."

"I hope so." She smiled. "The feeling is mutual."

After they left, Jennie decided to retire to her bedroom too, and kissed her mom and dad goodnight. She cozied up in bed, reliving the highlights of the day, the taste of Nick's kisses, and her emotional responses. She was conflicted, no doubt about it. She wanted to reach out and grasp a chance for happiness with greedy hands, and yet she also felt that Daniel deserved to be mourned and not forgotten. A new man in her life would need to understand and accept that, but it was a tall order to ask.

* * *

The week slid by. Between house-training Rasco and the excursions planned, each day had a new excitement. First day was with her sister and the kids watching the spectacular Disney on Ice. A few days later she took the kids to the science museum and to visit the Liberty Bell. She still had school friends that lived nearby and met up with them for a quick coffee and play dates with their children. One night they had a foot of new snow, and the cousins spent an afternoon tobogganing.

It was a happy and busy time, and it made Jennie eager to return to this city she loved. Leaving her parents made her sad, especially because life in Norfolk now held so little joy.

Her parents helped pack up her rental car, and stood waving to them as they backed out of the driveway. It was decided that they'd return for spring break, and Jennie would use that time to find a new home.

She'd talked to Nick every day, and on the first of January, he'd closed his restaurant, eager to show her his grandparent's home—and the park the girl's had heard so much about.

During the drive Brooke and Katie had kept up a lively conversation and Jennie had done her best to keep up with it, yet her heart was beating like a wild bird ready to take flight.

When she arrived in Heaven, she drove directly to Nick's, knowing he was waiting, and the SUV would be fine at the garage for a while longer. He stepped out to greet them before she reached the front door.

Katie and Brooke threw themselves into his arms, and he hugged them tight. Rasco jumped up and down, barking furiously for attention.

Nick laughed, and opened his arms to her, enveloping her in a big bear-hug. "I've missed you all," he said and chastely kissed her cheek.

"We had a wonderful week, but missed you too," she told him, so happy her smile stretched wide and she bounced on her toes.

Brooke tapped his arm. "Can we go in? I want to meet Sammy."

"Sure we can." He opened the door a few inches and a big dark nose poked out. The girls froze, wide-eyed. All they could see were two big eyes, a wet nose, and a lot of white fur.

218

"Is that him?" Katie asked. "He looks like a bear."

"He's a giant baby," Nick told the girls, holding the dog back and letting them through. Rasco pushed his way in too, and jumped on his best buddy, Sammy. Sammy bunted him back, and they chased each other around.

Nick was still at the half-open door, and Jennie had to brush by him. She made a point to stop at the moment of contact and look into his eyes. He winked at her, and her blood ran hot.

The girls stood in the entranceway, as if afraid to go further. Sammy was a little rambunctious and had almost knocked Brooke off her feet. "Will he bite?" she asked, quivering.

"No, he doesn't bite. He might slobber and give you wet kisses, but he loves little girls. He doesn't eat them."

Katie giggled. "Like the big bad wolf," she said. "I like your dog. Can I pet him?"

"In a few minutes, Katie. Right now they're kind of hyped up and need to settle down first." He opened the sliding back door for the dogs, hoping they'd burn off some energy outdoors.

"This is where you live?" Katie asked. "It's real cool." She looked at his coffee table. "I like that."

He grinned, looking enormously pleased, Jennie thought. "Thank you. I enjoy making things with my hands.. Wait until you see the house I'm renovating. It's going to be something when it's done. It has close to an acre, so lots of space for dogs and kids to run around."

"Oh?"

His eyes swept to Jennie's. "It'll make a great family home."

"Does it have a swing set?" Brooke asked.

"Not yet, but maybe one day." Nick didn't release Jennie's gaze. What was he saying?

"When it does, can we come and visit?"

"Brooke," Jennie warned.

"Anytime," Nick said. "You have an open invitation, and I hope you use it often."

"Can we, Mom?"

"Perhaps." She smiled, thrilled and delighted at how much her daughters liked Nick, and accepted him as part of their life—but that same thing frightened her.

"I'll just let the dogs back in, then we can go see the farm." He slid the door wide and called out, and the dogs came running.

Brooke stepped behind her mother, still afraid of the big white bear-like dog.

Katie put her hand out and Sammy licked it. She giggled. "He kissed my hand."

"I taught him to be a gentleman," Nick said. "And a gentleman always kisses a lady's hand."

Her eyes sparkled. "Really? Have you kissed Mom's hand?"

"Certainly. Want to see?" He bowed and made a swooping motion with his arm. "Milady?" Playing along, Jennie offered her fingers, which he took in his and kissed with a smacking noise. Then he pretended to nibble. "Hmm. Tastes good too."

Brooke howled with delight and both girls wanted their hands kissed. "Nibble on mine," Brooke told him. Nick obliged them both.

He had won their hearts forever, and unfortunately hers too.

She turned to him with tears in her eyes. "You are something else."

"In a good or bad way?"

"The best."

"Okay. On that note, let's go see this home that I hope will one day be yours."

Jennie's heart thundered. Did he mean he wanted her to buy it, or wanted her to move in as his wife?

Both possibilities excited her, but she longed for the second one to be true.

CHAPTER TWENTY-SIX

Once the dogs had food and water, they all slipped out the back door and jumped into Nick's Jeep. They traveled down country roads, tall Evergreens on either side. Rural farmyards or dense forest opened up to new developments of modern homes. What surprised her was the strip mall that seemed to come out nowhere.

He turned left off the main road and drove a quarter mile down a narrow street called Green Meadows Lane. Old farmhouses dotted the road. Wooden fences separated the property lines, and some might have been ten, fifteen acres with large barns.

"Dairy farms," he told her. "There's a horse ranch up here too."

"Horses?" Katie asked. "I love horses. Mom gave me riding lessons once. They said I was a natural." She smiled with pride. "What's a natural?"

"Means you were born to ride. If you come back up here this spring, I'll talk to the lady who owns it, and see if she can give you another lesson or two."

"But the cost..." Jennie said, and saw him shake his head.

"No cost. She's a customer—I'm sure she'll let the girls ride for free."

Jennie doubted that, but knew not to argue. He would likely want to pay.

They pulled into a long driveway lined with trees before opening up and she got her first glimpse of the farmhouse. Jennie's jaw dropped. "That's Grannie's house?" she said with a short laugh.

"Grannie's house, with a few improvements," Nick answered with a proud grin. "So you like it then?"

"It's magnificent." There were no other words to describe it. Beautiful stone and brick exterior, a massive picture window that must have been recently installed. "I was expecting something about half this size."

"The front and back porch are recent add-ons, as is the big window in the front."

"Have you ever considered being a contractor, or architect?" she teased.

"And give up cooking? Not a chance." He helped her out, and then the kids. "Besides this is hard work. I put in a lot of physical labor."

"I've seen your muscles at work," she said quietly, brushing by him, "and I'm impressed."

The girls ran to the house, squealing with excitement. Jennie walked with Nick at a slower pace, taking it all in. "This is beautiful, Nick. Even the fencing around the place, and the beautiful old trees? I can't believe you're thinking of selling it."

"I'm rethinking that. But it needs a family, a loving family. Don't you agree?" He squeezed her hand. "It's still not done, so I hope you won't be disappointed with the inside."

"I know I won't be. I'm already in love with it."

"Is that all you're in love with?" he asked, giving her a meaningful glance.

Her heart hummed in reply, but she left the question unanswered as the girls were waiting on the screened porch. They had jumped into the two Adirondack chairs and sat cross legged, as the seat was large and deep. "This is super cool," Katie said. "A chair for me and one for Brooke."

A small round table sat between the two chairs, and Nick had draped a flowered plastic tablecloth on top, anchoring it with a red poinsettia plant. He'd added a Holiday welcome mat for the front door. "There's a two car garage around the side," he told them, as he unlocked the door. "It leads to a huge patio deck which overlooks the large back yard."

He pushed the door open and they all entered. Jennie released a breath and put a hand on her chest. The foyer led to a large living room with gleaming wooden floors, and beautifully crafted carpets. There was a huge brick fireplace that took up most of one wall, and the others were painted a dark green. Bright pictures livened up the place, and natural light from the picture window flowed in.

He'd decorated simply with two large burgundy colored leather sofas, a large square wooden coffee table, and a wonderful built-in bookshelf against one entire wall. Another wall unit held a fifty inch TV and photos, and big heavy candles, and a few knickknacks that she was sure had come with the house—and belonged to his beloved Grandma.

"There's another fireplace in the master bedroom suite," he told her. "We'll see that later." He led her to the kitchen, and her eyes widened with surprise.

"Oh, my! This is gorgeous. Better than the one I have back home."

He grinned with pleasure. "Thanks. I know it's a selling feature and I figured I wanted to unload the place. Now—maybe not."

"Nice floors," she said, attempting to keep her heart rate in check. She felt like throwing her arms around him and showing him what he was doing to her insides. But the children were here, and in an hour or two they'd be on their way out of town, back to their life in Norfolk. Who knew if and when they'd see each other again?

"First thing I did was to remodel the kitchen. New steel appliances, granite counters, the flooring, window treatments and lighting." He shrugged. "I also expanded the windows to offer a better view of the landscaped backyard."

"Very nice. You did an amazing job." She walked around, amazed at how much counter space there was, and how attractively it was done—a rustic granite, a muted beige and brown backsplash on the walls below the rows and rows of polished Maplewood cabinets. Four bar stools sat next to the high counter, separating the work area from the rest of the kitchen. A cozy nook overlooked the patio and landscaped yard.

She walked to the window and looked out. "You did this patio deck?"

He stood next to her. "It took me a lot of time this summer, and I hired a couple of local boys to help." He draped a hand around her shoulder. "It's thirty feet wide, and twenty feet deep. The steps were the tricky part."

She shook her head. "Incredible. Not just a pretty face," she said smiling. "I see some very nice white birch trees and a weeping willow for shade." Her lips twitched as she shot him a glance. "What else do you have planned?"

"Well, I was going to leave it. But there's lots of room for an in-ground pool and a swing-set," he told her children.

"Yeah!" shouted Katie, and Brooke ran to the window to look out.

"Sounds wonderful. Show us more." She linked arms with him, and he walked them through a guest bedroom that he hadn't gotten around to fixing, and a small office with built in shelves that could use a little updating too.

"Here's the master bedroom," he said, letting the three of them enter first, then followed behind. "I put in a new king-sized bed, and the two reading chairs next to the window. And the lamp, and new plantation shades for the windows."

"It's gorgeous. It has a built-in closet, I see." Everything was perfect. As if he'd read her mind before they'd even met.

"Another important selling point," he added, rubbing his square jaw.

"And another closet that's a very good size. Lots of storage space too."

226

"I haven't had time to remodel the bathroom, but it will be done soon. And as you know I'm working on the one upstairs as well. The two bedrooms there are empty, but you can have a look. They'd make perfect kids' rooms."

"Where? Where are they?" Katie asked, and Brooke got set to run off.

"Up the staircase. Don't trip," he warned.

Jennie's heart soared at the sound of their laughter and excited shouts. She took a long look at Nick. "You pretty much thought of everything, didn't you?"

He lifted her hand and kissed the knuckles, rubbing his thumb over her skin. "Everything, but this." His eyes held hers and she saw moisture in their deep dark depth.

"What?" She raised a hand and cupped his cheek. What was wrong?

"I never expected you and the girls to walk into my life."

"We're leaving in an hour or two." She didn't want to start crying, too. "Does that help?"

He smiled and pulled her into his arms. "Smart ass. No, of course it doesn't help. It hurts like hell."

"Really?" She patted his muscular chest and grinned. "That makes me *very* happy."

"You are just cruel," he said and captured her mouth in a very ardent kiss. She swayed next to him, holding on to his shoulders when her knees buckled.

"What are you doing?" Her voice was breathy, low.

"Cementing something. I want you to know that this is not going away. It's real. I care very much for you, and even if you aren't going to be around, that won't change.

I want you and the girls in my life, and when you're ready, I hope you'll return. Come back to me."

"Nick…I want this too. But we can't make promises that we don't know we can keep."

"Just promise me one thing. That when you get home you remember me, everything we've said and done together. Examine your feelings and your heart. Don't let your head involved. It will say we haven't known each other long enough, and it's probably right. But our hearts know. And I'm trusting mine." He kissed her again. "I will wait for you no matter how long it takes. And that's my promise to you."

Her eyes misted up. "Oh, Nick. I feel it too. I do, and I hope it lasts. I think so. All I can promise is that we'll return for spring break. One way or the other, we will have our answer."

"That's the most I could hope for." He grabbed her hand and pulled her along. "Come on. I want you to see the girls' bedrooms."

The girls' bedrooms. Could this really be happening?

She ran up the stairs behind him, and the girls were standing in the middle of two sweet little rooms that once had been an attic. Slanted skylights and slanted ceilings made the rooms almost fairytale looking, as if they lived in a castle of their own. A small shared bathroom was added in the middle of the two separate, but identical rooms.

"Mommy, Mommy. Look at our bedrooms!" Brooke squealed, clapping her hands. "Aren't they perfect? My Princess bed will fit right here. And my bookshelves can be in that corner. And my toys all over the place."

Jennie laughed. "I'm sure that much is true." She glanced at Katie. "What do you think, honey? You like it too?"

"It's magical, Mommy. I'd like my own desk next to this window. Come look! See what I see."

Jennie stepped next to her daughter and glanced out. The room was so high they could see fields and more fields covered with snow. Rolling hills, a frozen pond, and beautiful trees and fences separated one property from another. The view was lovely and serene. Perhaps even magical. Katie was right.

"It is beautiful. Are you going to write your book here?" she asked softly, knowing that her daughter loved to read, and dreamed of writing the next Harry Potter.

"Yes, Mom. It's going to be called, "A story about Heaven.""

"Let's see, Mom?" Brooke pushed her way in. "It's so pretty, like a scene from Snow White! Maybe there's an evil witch or some nice elves. You could write about that."

Jennie blinked back tears. So many possibilities were contained in these walls. Dreams and happiness and hope—that this time their joy could endure like the home they stood in, for decades to come. "That sounds like a lovely story, honey."

Nick came over and wrapped his arms around all three girls. "Whatever you write, Katie, I'm sure that this story will have the happiest of all endings."

Jennie smiled up at him, and put her arm around his waist. "Yes. Why not? It's simply beautiful—a perfect place for new beginnings and happy endings."

Nick lifted her chin and kissed her, and the children threw their arms around them, and hugged them both.

This side trip to Heaven had given Jennie back her life.

She gazed into his eyes. "We will be back this spring, if we can wait that long."

"And I can always come visit you in between. I've decided to close Sunday and Monday's starting in January."

"That is the best news I've had all day."

"We will be seeing each other soon. I won't let you go."

"You won't have to, Nick. I know what I want. It's you."

THE END

A NOTE FROM THE AUTHOR

Thank you for reading A HEAVENLY CHRISTMAS, the first book in my new series! If you enjoyed this book, I'd appreciate it if you'd help others find it so they can enjoy it too.

• Lend it: This e-book is lending-enabled, so feel free to share it with your friends.

• Recommend it: Please help other readers find this book by recommending it to friends, readers' groups, and discussion boards.

• Review it: Let other potential readers know what you liked or didn't like about.

If you'd like to sign up for Patrice Wilton's newsletter to receive new release information, please visit PatriceWilton.com/contact

You can follow Patrice Wilton on Facebook and Twitter. Book updates can be found at PatriceWilton.com.

I would love to hear from you at patricewilt@yahoo.com.

OTHER BOOKS BY PATRICE WILTON

REPLACING BARNIE
book 1 in the Candy Bar series

WHERE WISHES COME TRUE
book 2 in the Candy Bar series

NIGHT MUSIC
book 3 in the Candy Bar series

REVENGE IS SWEET
single title Women's Fiction

CHAMPAGNE FOR TWO
single title Contemporary Romance

ALL OF ME
single title Women's Fiction

CATERED AFFAIR
single title Women's Fiction

A HERO LIES WITHIN
Contemporary Romance

HANDLE WITH CARE
Contemporary Romance

AT FIRST SIGHT
Contemporary Romance

SERENDIPITY FALLS
book 1 in a new romantic comedy series

WEDDING FEVER
book 2 in the Serendipity Falls series

LOVE STRUCK
book 3 in the Serendipity Falls series

TROUBLE IN VEGAS
book 1 in the Vegas series

A HOT NIGHT IN VEGAS
book 2 in the Vegas series

KISS ME SANTA
Holiday romance

PARADISE COVE
first book in my new series

PatriceWilton.com/books

Read on for a first look at PARADISE COVE. This new series, based in Islamorada in the Florida Keys will be available on Kindle Unlimited Jan.10th/2016. Reviews are especially important to authors, and I would love you to take a moment and leave a review for A HEAVENLY CHRISTMAS, and PARADISE COVE if you hopefully read it! Thank you so much, and I would love to hear from you.

Excerpt from
PARADISE COVE by Patrice Wilton
Copyright © 2015 by Patrice Wilton

Cardiac surgeon, Sean Flannigan lost his daughter from a rare leukemia—he can mend broken hearts, but his is beyond repair. Kayla Holmes and her sisters run a guest cottage in the Keys and their high spirits and positive energy are like a beacon of light that directs Dr. Sean's sailboat to Paradise Cove. Can Kayla's kind heart and generous spirit find a crack in Sean's armor, and her unconditional love be enough to heal his wounded heart?

CHAPTER ONE

Kayla Holmes ran into the front office where the cool air greeted her like a slap in the face. Summer in the Florida Keys was brutally hot, and yet the moment you escaped inside the chill factor was almost worse.

"Mom," she gasped, rubbing her bare arms. "Who is that man moving into Rhapsody? I saw him a minute ago bringing in fishing gear and several duffle bags. Looks like a week worth of supplies." The two bedroom cottage was near the beach; one of their best properties and priced accordingly.

Anna Jones smiled and peered over her sparkly reading glasses. "Why," she said with obvious pleasure, "that's our new guest. Sean Flannigan." Her dark eyes sparkled. "And it's not a week. He's staying for three months! Three months, and he paid up front." She rubbed her hands together, nearly bouncing in her excitement, though she lowered her voice and glanced toward the door to ensure they were alone. "This kind of revenue is just what we need to see us through the summer. Now if we just get another one or two long term guests, we wouldn't have to worry so much."

"Mom, you don't need to worry at all. Leave that to us girls. Our shoulders are broader than yours." Kayla gazed down at the petite five-foot two-inch woman who had somehow born three daughters that were all half a foot taller. Other than that, they shared the same flashing brown eyes, dark curly hair, and olive skin that tanned well—a gift from their Greek heritage.

"Instead of standing here talking to me, why don't you go welcome Mr. Flannigan? Help him settle in," Anna said with a teasing wink. "He's kind of cute. I noticed he wasn't wearing a wedding band, and he owns that big sailboat down at the marina." She came around the counter and gave her daughter a push. "Go on now. Introduce yourself." She brushed a speck of dirt from Kayla's tank top. "On second thought—maybe you should clean up first."

"I was weeding, Mom. I'm not going to change so that I can help our guest move in!" Kayla tossed her hair back, picking at a few stray strands that stubbornly clung to her damp cheeks. "He's in the Keys for heaven's sake—if he isn't used to a little sweat, he soon will be." She paused at the door. "Besides, I'm not looking for romance. Brian and I just broke up six months ago. I plan on enjoying my freedom."

"Well, a girl at your age should be married, not wanting her freedom. Whatever that means. You're not getting any younger. Thirty-one and still single! A beautiful girl like you. Where have all the good men gone?"

"You married them," Kayla answered with a laugh. "Well, two of them anyway."

"Yes, and buried them both too." Anna sighed, and waved her hands. "Off you go. Make sure Mr. Flannigan has towels and bathroom supplies." She removed her glasses with theatric flourish. "He's got an accent, which is kind of sexy."

"Sexy…really?" Kayla pretended shock, although her mother was only fifty-six and extremely youthful. "Where's he from?"

"I couldn't tell. Sean Flannigan sounds Scottish, but I don't think it's that." Anna gave Kayla another gentle push toward the door. "Go ask him and then we'll know for sure."

"Jeez, Mom. Don't be doing any matchmaking. Taylor, Brit and I will find our own men when we're ready." Kayla stood at the screened door, gazing out. "This place needs a lot of work."

When their step-dad died last fall, he'd left the small seaside resort to his stepdaughters and his wife. It was supposed to be his retirement plan, but a sudden heart attack stole that from him.

"I know, honey, and I'm glad for the work. It gives me something positive to do instead of moping around." Anna put her glasses back on, blinking against tears.

"Of course it does." She squeezed her mom's hand. "We're in this together." Kayla mentally went through a top priority list of things to do. "First we'll get the grounds spruced up, and a new deck for the pool, then I'd like to paint the units before fall. It needs a clean, refreshed make-over. The sooner the better."

Paradise Cove Cottages consisted of twelve efficiency cabins with small kitchens, a living area, and a covered patio to enjoy the view. The larger units faced the ocean, whereas the one-bedrooms were grouped around the pool next to the beach. All needed updating.

"Doesn't mean you girls can't find time to meet some nice men, does it?"

"That's exactly what it means." She smiled to soften the words. Her mom had loved being married and wanted to see her daughters with husbands and children of their own. Kayla wasn't opposed to the idea, but she could wait. "We have plenty to do here that will keep us busy. I'm sure not going to chase after romance. I'm happy to wait until it finds me."

Anna put her hand on Kayla's arm. "Fine, just don't go running away from it, either."

"I don't plan to. It's just on the back burner." She'd dated a guy in Philadelphia, a sales manager with a big company, working himself up the corporate ladder. It had been fun and games for awhile, but he was more interested in moving ahead than moving in with her. They'd called it quits when Kayla told him she was moving to the Keys.

"Don't let that burner wait too long. Time has a way of slipping by, and you need to grab happiness when you can."

"I will, Mom. Just as soon as we get this place up to snuff. Allan would want it that way. You know he would."

Her mother blinked back tears. "I know. He's up there looking down on us, and we will make him proud. We will." She sniffed and smiled. "Off you go now. I've got to set up an appointment for the Conley family to go snorkeling this afternoon."

"I'll take over the office at noon—give you a break. Why don't you go into town? Get away from here for a few hours."

"I might do that. Oh, what do you think of The Good Life as a name?"

"Name for what?" Kayla asked. "A boat?"

"No. Our cabin."

"It's fine, Mom, but let's hold off on that until we can get them all redone. It's just not a priority." Each cabin had a wooden plaque above the door. The previous owner had called one Rhapsody, the next, Serenity, then Tranquility, and finally Harmony. The smaller units were Bliss, Happy Days, Smooth Sailing, Hooked & Baited, Hibiscus, Bougainvillea, The Palms, and then there was their own cottage. Passions.

"That's probably best since we want to paint all the units anyway," her mother agreed. "But us four unmarried women living in a cabin called Passions just doesn't seem right. What will people think?"

"Who cares? One look at this place and they'll know we're not running a brothel." The cottages were set back from Overseas Highway, the one and only road that took visitors from the mainland to the Keys. A dirt path lined with scattered palm trees, scrub brush and pines led to the office where her mother and all three sisters rotated shifts. They had a pool, some swings and a couple of bikes for the children, and rented out kayaks. Not glamorous, but family friendly. "Right now we need to stick to our business plan."

"All right, all right." Anna walked back to the desk and sat down before the computer. "See you later, dear. Don't forget our guest."

"I won't." Kayla closed the door behind her so her mother could enjoy the air conditioning. Then she headed towards the cabin on the beach to give Mr. Flannigan a warm welcome. Three months rent would go a long way right now. Paid in cash. How unusual.

"Hey," she called, watching the man's backside as he hauled a large duffle bag toward the cabin. *Not bad.* "Welcome to Paradise Cottages."

Turning around as if startled, he dropped the bag near the porch and stuffed his hands into his khaki shorts. He nodded at her and mumbled, "Good morning."

She tried to identify the accent, but failed. South African? Australian?

He was tall and thin, probably about fortyish, with sandy brown hair that curled around his ears, and a four o'clock shadow at ten a.m. His features were ordinary, not too big, not too small. Kayla wouldn't call him handsome, but that might be due to the scowl on his face.

"And a good morning to you." She came forward with a big smile and a welcoming hand, wishing she'd taken the time to change out of her dirty shirt. "I'm Kayla Holmes. You met my mother, Anna, and no doubt you'll meet my sisters soon. We're very glad to have you with us and want to make your stay as comfortable as possible. If there is anything you need, please don't hesitate to call. We live in the first cottage, Passions, and we're available 24/7."

Kayla's cheeks warmed as she stumbled over the name of their cottage. Maybe her mother was right, and the name change needed to be moved up the list.

He didn't smile or take her extended hand. "Sean Flannigan." His brown eyes flickered over her, then shifted away as he inched toward his cabin door. "I don't need much." He pointed at the marina. "I've been staying on my boat for the past month. I'll be fine once I settle in."

He spoke in short sentences that didn't welcome further conversation, but Kayla soldiered on. "Yes, well, there's a small grocery store a few blocks down, within walking distance. We can book tours through the Everglades, or get you a reservation at any of the local restaurants. We also offer drives into town. Just let us know you're interested and when one of us is free, we'd be happy to take you wherever you want to go. All part of the service we provide."

His expression didn't change. There was no warmth in his eyes, just wariness, as though he might have something to hide.

"Nice of you to offer, but I don't need anything. If I do, I'll let you know." He had one hand on the doorknob.

Maybe he was a drug runner or arms smuggler. Something was off about him and it wasn't just the accent. *She stepped closer, wondering what he had in those duffle bags. "You don't need groceries or anything?"*

"I've come here for some solitude." He didn't move from the porch. His knuckles tightened on the knob.

"Solitude. Got it!" She jammed her hands into her shorts. "You want anything to go along with that solitude? A good book? Some nice music? Tequila?" She gave him a bright smile, hoping for a little one in return.

She backed away from his pointed look. "Okay. One last thing before I get out of your hair—we have happy hour every day at the pool. Four to six. Mom makes the best drinks in town. Guaranteed to give you a buzz. Not that you want one. Solitude and buzzes don't really go together." She squinted, reflecting on it for a second.

His jaw clenched.

"Or maybe they do," she babbled on. "Not sure. Anyway, today her secret weapon for putting a smile on your face will be Mango Daiquiri's. If you get away from your solitude for an hour you'll meet my sisters and our other guests. We don't have many. But there's a nice family from Ohio. And a cute couple on their honeymoon."

He walked into the cabin and shut the door behind him.

Well, of all the nerve! She'd only tried to be friendly. What was his problem? Rude and secretive. No one could live under her nose, especially in Paradise Cove, and *Rhapsody* no less, and do something sinister. They didn't have a Sinister name plate, and they sure in hell weren't about to put one up.

* * *

"What a pushy woman," Sean mumbled as he tossed his duffle bags on the counter. He unzipped the heaviest one, taking out cans of soup and stews he'd been practically living on for the last few weeks. Now with a proper kitchen he could buy some fresh produce and good steaks. Fry up the last of the fish in his cooler while it was still edible. He enjoyed cooking, but he preferred putting in the effort when he had someone to cook for. Those days were gone.

"Happy hour? I don't think so." The short interaction with Kayla left him frazzled and certain he wasn't ready for human company. And yet, he'd gotten lonely on the boat. He'd left Boston five weeks ago, with no particular destination in mind. He'd needed to clear his head and mend his heart. As a doctor he knew that those two particular areas were mostly untreatable.

The six months prior to his exodus from Boston had been spent in a two-bedroom condo not far from the hospital where he worked. It hadn't been luxurious, but it had been convenient after the divorce. He'd continued on auto pilot, closing down emotionally so that he felt nothing. No pain. No heartache. No regrets.

Those had seeped in later. The divorce was a direct result of the death of their precious ten-year-old daughter, who'd lost the fight to lymphoblastic leukemia. His wife blamed him for not being able to save Sara. Punishing him had given Laura a reason to get out of bed each morning. He understood that, and didn't blame her any. It had helped her survive something that no parent should ever have to face.

Why had the good Lord decided that little Sara was the one to go? Had it been her bright smile, her love and joy, her pure heart? Had she been too good for this world? Did Sara look down upon them now, and see how bitter they'd become? How her death had caused a rift so deep and wide, that it could never be healed? He hoped not. Instead, he liked to think she was upstairs amusing the angels with her silly jokes and cheerful ways.

Sara had died just over a year ago and the remembered pain lanced through him, nearly bringing him to his knees in the tiny kitchen of the cabin. Sean knew it would never go away, but he was starting to remember his daughter with good memories too, not just the endless surgeries, the dozen rounds of chemo, or her weak body as she lay dying in a hospital.

He sank into a chair and looked out the window. Children played on the beach—one was running with a kite, the other had a bucket and a shovel and was making a sand castle.

The image made him smile sadly as he remembered the past, but at least he was strong enough now to take out the precious moments he'd been given with his daughter and look at them with love, instead of just anger and hurt. Far worse than the pain, would be to forget one single minute of Sara's young life.

Two women in big sunhats and shorts over their swimsuits hiked the beach, gesturing with their hands as they talked. He'd seen them plenty of times from the deck of his boat, or as he'd fished from the pier. He knew they were Kayla's sisters, and that the three women ran this place with their mother.

He told himself they weren't the reason he'd chosen to stay in Paradise Cove. Sean had no interest in getting to know these happy, laughing women so full of life, so carefree, as though they'd never faced tragedy.

Yet, something had drawn him here besides the convenience of the marina next door. Was it loneliness, he wondered? He'd been divorced for less than a year, but alone much longer than that. Was it human nature to crave the solace of other strangers, the sounds of voices? If so, why had Kayla's cheerfulness nearly sent him running?

He didn't understand himself anymore. He was clever. Brilliant, some thought. But he couldn't answer why he was here anymore than he could find a cure to save his baby girl. What good was intelligence or medical knowledge if it failed you in the end? He was the same as anybody else. Not smarter, and certainly not better. He bled. He felt. He cried. He was just a man.

Sean got out of the chair, wiped damp tears off his face with a paper towel from the dispenser on the counter and continued to unpack his bags. Instant noodles went into the cupboard, along with peanut butter and jelly, and half a loaf of bread. Kayla had mentioned a grocery store nearby. If he was going to be here for three months, he should probably rent a car. He hoped he wouldn't regret the impulse to stay awhile.

He sniffed the milk, rearing back at the sour smell, then dumped it down the sink, and the small coffee creamer too. The six pack of Corona fit in the fridge and he stuck a bottle of scotch on the side counter, under the cupboard where he'd seen the glasses.

Shoulders slumped, he felt drained of energy. The simple motion of unpacking had zapped most of his strength. Previously he'd been an active man, but living in cramped quarters for the past month had atrophied him. A walk would do him good. He felt stiff inside and out.

He took a long hot shower, enjoying the full power of the spray and having room to move after the confined space on the boat. Then he dressed in an old but favorite pair of jeans, a clean blue tee with a fish head on the back, and headed out. He stopped at the office for directions, but instead of the attractive middle-aged lady, Kayla stood at the bookshelves by the desk. They had tourist information on the top half, and used books on the bottom. She was adding one to the collection. He glanced at the title. The Seductress and the Rake. *His wife had enjoyed historical romances as well.*

"Hey," she said with a sunny smile. "How can I help you, Mr. Flannigan?"

He hadn't been called "Mister" in a long time. But the "doctor" title seemed inappropriate, and he didn't need any formality. Matter of fact, he wanted to be "average Joe" and stay invisible. "Call me Sean."

Why did her bright smile illicit such a negative reaction from him? Sean could tell it was genuine. He'd seen her smiling and singing to herself earlier when he'd walked from the marina to get a room. She'd worn a big straw hat that covered most of her face. He'd wondered what the heck she had to sing about. Had to be a hundred degrees in the sun, and she was working hard, cleaning the walkway from the pool that led to the beach. Bending over and pulling weeds between the wooden steps, trimming the wild grass that grew along the sides. She'd been sweating buckets, but catching sight of him, she'd wiped her forehead with her arm, grinned and waved.

Even at her worst, he knew she was a stunning looking woman. Yet he hadn't returned the wave. Instead, he'd plowed on, head down pretending he hadn't seen her.

"Sean, then. We're all curious about your accent." She smiled again, darn near blinding him. "Where are you from, if you don't mind me asking?"

He did mind, but he answered anyway. "Boston. For the past twenty-five years." Conversation seemed forced to him now. For a month he'd drifted alone on his boat, only stopping for gas and food. He didn't have much to say anymore. Not to strangers, not to family or friends. He didn't want their words of sympathy or to see a look of sadness in their eyes. Even a light-hearted chat with a pretty woman couldn't muster any appeal. He was part of the walking dead. Just no one knew it.

"Before that," she persisted. "It's not a Scottish brogue, is it?"

"Nope. Born in Australia." He tried a smile which felt stiff and unnatural. More of a grimace. "Moved to the States when I was sixteen," he mumbled, shifting his feet, eager to get away.

"Do you say things like "dinky-di?" She laughed and brushed back her dark brown curly hair. "I worked at a Hyatt in Philly, and we had a rugby team in. I heard them use it a few times."

He scowled. "Not if I can help it." Must have been the work that she'd done for a hotel chain that made her so damn customer-service oriented. Probably should have stayed on his boat where there was peace and quiet, only the occasional squawking of a seagull flying by.

Ignoring his bad manners, she walked across the office to the small refrigerator that held cold waters, taking one for herself, offering him another. "So, what brought you here? To South Florida?"

He accepted the water, uncapped it and took a big drink. "Look, I just stepped in to find out where the nearest market is, not to answer twenty questions." After a few more slugs of the water, he placed it on the counter. He knew he was being rude, but she seemed damned determined not to leave him alone. Enough was enough. "Appreciate the water though," he said, taking a step towards the door.

"I'm sorry. I'm just trying to be friendly. You want to keep to yourself, it's all the same to me."

He shrugged his shoulders, hoping to shed his guilt. "I just don't want to talk about myself, that's all."

"Fair enough." She pointed at the door. "When you leave here, follow the dirt road to the street, then turn right."

Sean shot her a look of apology. It wasn't her fault he couldn't stand to be around people. She was just doing her job, and his rudeness was not to be excused. "I'm sorry for jumping down your throat. Got some things to work out. Talking doesn't help."

Clearing her throat, she said, "It's okay." She kept her eyes averted. "There's a small general store about three blocks from here. You want a better selection, you've got to go a couple of miles. Big supermarket down the way a bit." She glanced at her watch, refusing to look at him. "If you can wait an hour, Mom will be back. She can drive you."

"Thanks, but no. The walk will do me good." He opened the door and the heat hit him like an open furnace. Walking far in this humidity might not be such a great idea. He glanced back. "I was thinking about renting a car while I'm here."

"Good idea." She stood, as if waiting for him to say something else. Letting him know she thought he was a Grade A jerk.

"Can you make the arrangements or is there a place in town?"

Kayla nodded. "I can look after it. No problem," and she gave him that blasted smile once again. Like she just couldn't help being ridiculously happy.

"Thanks." He turned and started toward the road ahead, heading for the shade of the large palms.

Kayla called out, "Don't forget happy hour. You'll be back by then, I hope."

"Wouldn't miss it for the world," he answered, shaking his head. He had zero intention of showing up to drink girly drinks with a bunch of strangers. Maybe he could find a dark bar, a beer and a burger, and hang around until the damn thing was over.

"Perfect." Kayla said in her cheerful voice.

He left without a backward glance.

THE END

Printed in Great Britain
by Amazon